Martinis & Bikinis

A Novel

By
Andrew Cotto

Prologue

The idea, like so many of massive effect and modest intention, came in an instant. The fact that it involved an anachronistic actor of unique swagger and fortitude as well as one of the world's most recognized yet private persons, a woman of English elegance and California beauty, surely inspired the madness that would follow in its wake and set fire to a lumpen nation with a fetish for celebrity, sex and scandal. And so it began with an idea that was actuated with a photograph and abetted by technology, dispirit accomplices, clandestine maneuverings, exquisite branding, and an epic humiliation that would leave a large portion of America burning and the whole country choking on its own foul dust. And so it began...

Part I

Jack Flaherty adjusted his eyes to the overwhelming sunshine, the overwhelming everything of Los Angeles: the cars and cachet on boutique-lined boulevards; palm trees and lush vegetation making everything seem exotic yet pastoral. The sky shimmering and blue as blown glass. Jack had forgotten the beauty of LA, the ambiance. The women. How ample and beautiful they were, as if they'd fallen from trees like the oranges and lemons that landed softly on the manicured lawns of Santa Monica. Feeling the spell of its Utopian mist surround him, Jack began to wonder why, nearly ten years ago, he had left California, until turning onto Ocean Boulevard and seeing, before the sandy expanse and endless ocean, the human fruit gathered below the Palm trees, rotting and ignored, buttressed only by their corroded belongings. The conflicted nature of California came back to him as he rubbed his stubbly skull and squinted through his shades.

Back on Wilshire Boulevard, Jack inched towards the valley, reminding him of the primary problem he had with LA: the traffic. As a city boy, and one of considerable height, he despised traveling by car and remembered the daily aggravation and physical discomfort he experienced in his LA days, relying on the cluttered avenues and choked freeways to get virtually anywhere. He damned the detour he'd taken from LAX to see the ocean and the building on Wilshire where he had lived after dropping out of USC, and thought of stopping at an intersection pay phone, backed by familiar strip malls of white plaster with neon lights in storefront windows offering messages / take-out food / liquor / mailings / DIY divorce. He thought of finally investing in a cell phone – ending his status as one of the last men on earth without one - though the idea of constant connectivity challenged his independent nature. He eyed the rusted pay phone kiosk across the avenue that seemed more like a time piece relic than a utilitarian device, though sometimes payphone lines still worked, and he needed to make a call, since his lateness was guaranteed and he hadn't even entered the freeway yet, but he thought better of having to switch lanes to exit and re-enter traffic more hostile than slow, especially after news on the radio announced the shooting of a motorist in yet another vehicular dispute on the 405 freeway. The report had implied the murder may have been gang related, but Jack had his doubts: The trigger-man could have just as easily been the unusual suspect in the next lane, pounding the steering wheel of his Prius and screaming into his headset. Traffic related violence had reached epidemic proportion in this sweltering American autumn of the 21st century.

Los Angeles was definitely hotter than Jack remembered. The heat more intense, even stifling the ocean breeze. Temperatures averaged in the high 90s throughout much of the recent years, with the summer months tipping 110 for weeks at a time. This was the new normal for Southern California where high temperatures and drought baked the land and made it feel like the edges of the earth were curling up. While the Northeast and coastal South were ravaged by frequent hurricanes, and tornadoes tormented the drought-stricken Midwest and Southern inlands, Southern California has essentially become a residential desert, an extension of Palm Springs. The city of Los Angeles was hot and dry and choked by dangerous levels of smog. The highways were a war zone. The hills a fire hazard. But the patina of fabulous, of glamour and glitz, remained, though its superficiality seemed as transparent as thinning Arctic ice.

Jack powered up the windows of his rented and new-smelling four-door, sealing off the hot air and the steamy pollution it carried. He scanned satellite radio for a new station while crawling to his 3:00 meeting in Burbank.

"Afternoon Angelinos and Americanos," a raspy, snarky-effeminate voice muttered a script that spilled through Jack's door panel speakers. "It's time to put four on the floor, if you know what I mean, and welcome the king of the afternoon drive, the one re-writing the rules of radio, Bernie......Golden."

A bombastic rock song followed on the heels of the tepid introduction.

The voice-over was familiar, though dated, but Jack had never heard of Bernie Golden or his eponymous radio program until noticing a billboard a ½ mile (or ½ hour) back, high above the sprung tops of the palm trees, featuring the cartoon depiction of a shock of red hair between two shapely legs jutting from under a table, with a radio microphone on top and a voluptuous blonde behind, in headphones, reclined ecstatically in a chair with the caption "Oh, Bernie!" coming from her open mouth. The caption across the top of the billboard read: Get Down with The G-Man Weekdays from 3:00 to 6:00 on 101 FM – KBAL.

"What? I don't pay you enough, Leonard?" An urgent voice with a slight western twang asked after the introduction music faded. "I mean, come on, how about some enthusiasm, all-right?"

"No, Bernie," the taxed voice from the intro responded, "You don't pay me enough. You couldn't possibly pay me enough."

A thick, dopey voice freighted by arrogance and heft chimed in. "Then what are you here for anyway?"

"Because I need the money, Sidney, and this so-called program needs a professional, someone with a little common sense, to temper you buffoons. You know that. Everyone knows that."

"Yeah, well lighten up, anyway," Sidney responded.

"I'm light," Leonard answered. "Don't start with me today, Sidney."

"And everyone knows you're light," Sid's big voice countered, followed by a new voice, snappy and Latino, snickering. A track played of a man moaning, followed by the sound of a long fart. More snickering.

"Fantastic," Leonard waxed sarcastic. "Homophobia is just so in these days."

"Enough already, Sid, " Bernie intervened, laughing as well. "I gotta take a leak, so let's get started with today's Golden Shower. Who's our douche-du-jour?

Silence ensued.

"What?" Bernie wondered out loud. "No one has nothing for me today? No slutty starlet caught in a compromising position? No cellulite, crotch shots, cleavage or tramp stamps on display? No lame-ass actor caught doing the walk of shame? It's your guys job to comb the tabloids for something every day for me to relieve myself on. It's part of the show."

"Sorry G-Man," Sid offered solemnly, reverentially. "We usually do this later, so we got time to go through the tabs during the breaks. I got nothing right now."

The Latino voice mumbled something indecipherable, followed by seconds of silence, which seemed much longer on radio.

"Don't look at me!" Leonard finally demanded. "I don't play that absurd game."

"Come on, Lenny," Sid countered. "You invented the douche-du-jour."

"Please. I just informed you imbeciles of how to say "shower" in French. That is my only contribution to your pathetic ritual."

"I still, to this day, have a hard time believing that the French call the shower a douche," Sid admitted with a chuckle. "What it ever do to them?"

"Yeah, mang," the Spanglish-inflected voice entered. "No wonder they don't bathe that much, you know?"

"Oh, please," Leonard countered, "the average French citizen has more culture in the tips of their pinkies than the lot of you have combined in all of your person's put together. If any of you would bother..."

"OK, drop the soap and get off the box," Bernie interrupted to resume his authority. "And if none of you other apparent queers has anything to offer today in terms of a shower guest, we'll have to go with our de facto douche…Angelica Lightman."

A drum rolled into a cymbal splash, followed by the sound of paper being torn then an unfastened zipper and the sound of urination.

Jack switched off the radio as the toilet flushed.

*

A controversial presidential election had consequences. The new government went right to work gutting oversight and control of the nation's media.

- NPR, PBS and all other public broadcasting was eliminated.

- Control of the airwaves was ceded to the private sector where it was bought up quickly by foreign corporations.

- The FCC was reduced to a toothless team of four political appointees doling out meager fines for major indiscretions which inspired a rebirth of ribald talk radio.

- Copyright laws were watered down to the point of uselessness; a wave of knock-off and dirt cheap electronic imports flooded America, leaving 95% of the population 12 years of age and older with smartphones. Apple was relegated to a boutique brand.

Artists of recognition fled in droves. Run off by dwindling opportunities, diminished respect, media stalking and relentless hacking of their personal information. Ex-pat colonies sprouted up in Vancouver, Bulgaria, Mexico City and Buenos Aires. Starving artists and ambitious hipsters were priced out of the major cities and began gentrifying rural towns and blighted urban areas. The Bronx became the new Brooklyn. Camden was in vogue.

And under these conditions, the anachronistic actor Jack Flaherty had earlier in the year made his first film, a supporting role in the rare movie of thematic depth. And he had this particular day traveled from his hometown of Boston to Los Angeles, where he was once a college athlete and an aspiring actor, for a few days to meet with his agent to discuss the film's forthcoming promotion, if he could survive the detour from the airport that left him mired in freeway traffic, more hostile than slow, and make it to Burbank on time for LA standards.

*

"Hello Jack," Mona November sang as he arrived for his appointment more than two hours late. She tilted her head and smiled. Mona was just past-her-prime pretty, with the calling card of plastic surgeon on her wide eyes, pouting lips, and gravity-defying breasts sealed in a sleeveless silk blouse, tied tightly round her narrow waist by a thick belt. Her hair was streaked straw and amber, the colors of a leopard, pulled up into a tidy bun pierced by a chopstick.

"Mona?" Jack asked approaching, taking in her appearance, then the demure hand offered.

"What?" she asked, acknowledging his confusion. "You were expecting someone different?"

"Yeah, well," he said, stuffing his long arms into front pockets of faded jeans. "I just assumed, you were, you know, more mature."

"I'm 37, Jack," Mona said, hands on hips in a Wonder Woman pose. "That is quite 'mature' around here."

"Oh," he laughed. "So what's that make me?"

She looked him up and down.

"I put you at 28," she said nodding. "And you're a man, so don't worry."

"Good to know," he said, feigning relief, as she sat back down. "Nice to meet you, finally. Sorry I'm late."

"My pleasure, and don't worry. This is LA. All etiquette died with Walt Disney," she said, staring up at his angled face, more severe from below than in the head shots and dailies she had studied. He had a sickle-shaped scar under his chin and was one of the few men she had encountered who actually looked more handsome without hair. She continued her stare until the phone rang. "Sit. I'll tell Spence your here."

"Berman Agency," she answered, after carefully arranging the headset then pushing a button with a red nail. Jack had spoken frequently with Mona November on the phone, far more than he had with Spence Berman. He loved her movie star name, and her active involvement in his affairs gave Jack the impression that she was for more than an assistant.

The reception area was wood-paneled and windowless, covered in framed photos like a big-time steak house, with Spence Berman, in every picture, as the would-be Maitre'D in a monkey suite, mugging for the camera among smiling faces. Jack was nearly swallowed by the leather couch, before sitting up on the edge and rubbing his sinewy left arm. He was wearing jeans and a weathered black T-shirt, and wishing he had changed, maybe even showered, but Spence had insisted he come straight from the airport, and the detour to Santa Monica had made him late enough.

"Anything to drink?" Mona mouthed while covering the mouthpiece.

"No thanks," Jack mouthed back.

She smiled, turned her eyes away, then back.

Jack stood and began surveying Wall 1 of the photo exhibit: separate shots of Spence posed with mostly-dated movie stars with a smattering of a few contemporary ones in between. A younger version of Mona flanked the celebrity sandwiched in some older shots; in other, more recent ones, she was missing. He wondered if Spence ever took the tuxedo off.

"Hey," Spence came beaming from behind his door, adjusting the cuffs of his tux. "Did you walk from the airport? You couldn't afford a car service after the check I sent you?"

Jack stayed still as Spence approached, gold crowns lining the runway of his salesman-smile as he crossed the room to shake hands. He hadn't seen Spence since signing on with his agency a year ago at a meeting in New York. Gray had slipped from his crinkly hair into his trimmed beard, and he appeared even shorter from Jack's stretched perspective, his jowls more wolf-like, and he hunched a little now, stooped across the collar bones, though his eyes were still full of energy, passion for himself and "the business."

"Come in, come in," Spence led him by the arm. "Did Mona offer you something? You want some water, tea, juice, there's a juice bar downstairs – I could send the girl."

"She offered," Jack said, while being led through the wide doorway. "I'm fine."

Mona November drummed her nails on the desk, and plotted.

*

Jack had a seat on a large leather couch posited in front of Spence's wide desk in his spacious office. The sun light gathered in the windows, blurring the smoggy foothills of the Verdugo Mountains just beyond the tops of nearby buildings.

Spence went into the adjoining bathroom and clipped his nose hair while making small talk about Jack's flight from Boston.

Seeking decorum, Jack looked around the spacious office at bookshelves lined with scripts, awards, and even more framed photos. If the reception area was a tribute to Spence's Hollywood stature, the office was a shrine to his best known client. A framed movie poster of Il *Bel Paese* with a signature squiggled across the bottom; another framed poster, of the remake of *Some Like It Hot*, with Angelica Lightman in the Marilyn Monroe role. Photo after enlarged photo of Spence and Angelica Lightman at various events, glamorous locations; you would think they were father-daughter if she was clearly not from the same gene-pool, and if he seemed as interested in her as being photographed with her.

"You ever met Angelica Lightman?" Jack asked as Spence returned from his nose pruning; he looked stunned for a moment before breaking into a wide grin.

"Very funny, you rascal," he said, wagging a finger. "What can I say. I'm so proud of her."

"How long have you been her agent?"

"Her whole life!" he beamed. "Her mother, God rest her heart, was my first client. I had brought her to the studio I ran back then. She was just a kid herself, and we made some great pictures together, great pictures, but when our deal was up, the big guys offered her something I couldn't touch, not back then, at least, so, what was I going to do? I gave her my blessing to go, of course, which she did, under one condition." Spence leaned back for effect waiting for the prompt.

Jack said nothing.

"She insisted that I come with her," Spence delivered the punch line, jolting into upright position, poking his desktop, "to represent her and her interests, and that's how I became an agent." He sat back, clasping his arms around the back of his head.

"What about her?" Jack motioned with his head towards a picture of the daughter with mother: a premature adolescent hugging her could-be-older-sister, both tanned and filling bikinis, in the rolling tide of an exotic beach at dusk.

"I got Angie her first spot at 7 – even then, she had more talent than anyone on the set," he nodded. "This kid can really act, always could – I guess that's what happens when a director and a starlet have a kid, someone with looks who can really act. They don't make them like her anymore."

Jack found a picture of the father, austere and bald on top with a neatly trimmed beard, holding his daughter proper, by the waist, as she poses for yet another photo on the night she won her Oscar, in a role he had directed. He looks merely pleased. Smug. Jack had heard the father, a legendary English director, sure to be a "Sir" someday, was difficult, and that there was some sort of rift after the awards. He knew about the book the mother wrote shortly before her death – a tell-all that told too much, at least about the ex-husband. He had seen a few of the daughter's films, and he had liked them. He knew she hadn't worked in a while, thought he recalled something about her quitting the business a while back, and he hadn't heard a word about Angelica Lightman in as long as he could remember until earlier that day during that asshole radio show where the host had presumably pissed on a picture of her. Jack thought of it as a funny coincidence that he was now staring at her picture, and that they shared an agent. But he also had no idea, at the moment, that Angelica Lightman was the reason he was sitting where he was, and that their adventure together would begin that night.

*

Jack searched through his duffle bag for a fresh shirt. He tried on one, then another – throwing the discarded items into the trunk of the new-smelling four-door in the subterranean parking lot of Spence's office building. He was thrown by what Spence had told him only minutes before and left scrambling for a decent appearance. He sniffed under his arm after feeling the coolness of moisture collect. And then he stopped still, as if slapped in back of the head.

This is bullshit, he thought. Some sort of old-school Hollywood initiation rite, where Spence and some of his dusty cronies would come bounding out from behind some cars, laughing and slapping backs after watching him panic in the parking lot. "Welcome to Hollywood kid!" they would bellow. "And you really thought Angelica Lightman wanted to meet you!"

Jack packed up the scattered articles and climbed in the car. He would see for himself about this situation before going through anymore gymnastics. He put the car in gear and merged onto Alameda Avenue. The address stamped on a pack of matches seemed doubtful, another Hollywood trope. He knew the area, but had never heard of this place on the pack of matches. He rubbed at his head and considered the possibilities while driving through the magic of twilight.

Jack questioned Mona about this supposed meeting after Spence had rushed off to his event. Of course she knew that place, and, of course, the meeting was legit: She had arranged it herself. Why? She knew, but couldn't answer. It was a surprise. A surprise? She had given Jack a brand new iphone and programmed the address into the GPS. Jack took the phone, reluctantly, but told her not to bother with the GPS, so she pulled out a book of matches with a name stamped on the outer flap. She told him a name that she wrote on the inner flap. Mona tossed Jack the matchbook and called him a "dinosaur" as he walked out of the office towards his car in the parking lot.

No way, Jack thought, standing beside his car and feeling stupid. He barely knew these people, Mona November and Spence Berman, and he was entrusting them with his career? With his dignity? They had paid for his trip, and put him up at the Beverly Hilton. *Strange fucking town*, Jack reassured himself. *Strange fucking people.* He remembered another reason he had left LA: the people. There was a bizarre vacuity that he found unsettling. People who knew the names of assistant directors on minor films but not that of any Supreme Court Justices. People who didn't seem to know your name after numerous meetings. People who intimately used only the first names of people they'd never met.

Jack, having left the confines of Burbank, shifted off Sunset Boulevard, with its tourist veneer and T-shirt franchises, into the Hollywood Hills, then onto Mulholland Drive, a serpentine ridge that split the valley from the coast. Dusk was settling in a riot of pastels, and he was above the lights that twinkled below, looking down from space as trees whisked past his open window.

Jack wound through the serpentine roads, troubled by the well-lit houses with tennis courts in back, elevated above the gorge by stilts the length of a football field. Imagine playing tennis, maybe just about to serve for the match, when the big one struck? There wouldn't be enough yellow balls down there to break that fall. He relaxed, gliding down the hill into Pacific Palisades, where the dry stench of cluttered urban pockets had been exchanged for a salty breeze. He remembered from a map he had bought back in college, after just arriving in LA, that Tom Hanks, his all-time favorite actor, lived around there, maybe even in one of the understated houses, separated by cypress and palm trees, along the easily accessible roads that still sold for well into the 7-figures. Nah, Hanks had a mansion, but he'd probably prefer to have neighbors, if he hadn't already abandoned LA like most everyone else of talent and integrity had.

The matchbook read "Blue Roses" and Jack, refusing to attempt the iphone GPS, had to actually stop and ask directions to find the hidden establishment, back off a side street, down a gravel road, through a forest of umbrella pines. The wooden restaurant was poorly lit, a bark-colored cabin, with only a gaslight out front, and small, white bulbs tracing the two rectangular windows on either side of the wooden door. A smattering of cars were parked in front. Jack slowly went down the road, tires crunching gravel as he approached. He stepped out, taking a satisfied breathe of the pines that surrounded the remote opening, thinking that if this was a hoax, at least they'd sent him to a cool place. And he loved the name. He walked inside without changing his shirt.

Through the threshold was a long bar, with a few patrons sipping brown liquor from beveled glasses. A thick, bow-tied bartender with mutton chops and cauliflower ears leaned into the side neatly lined with bottles, watching a rugby match on TV. His shoulders were as wide as an ax handle. The bartender and the patrons ignored Jack as he approached the far end of the bar, leaning sideways into the wooden expanse. Still suspicious, he opened the matchbook again, then called out to the bartender, "Wally?"

The booze sippers looked over, and the bartender straightened up.

"Whad'you call me, mate?" he asked in an industrial English accent.

Jack stared at him for a few seconds, unable to make a reading. He flicked open the matchbook at his hip, and read the name again. He studied the imposing bartender and grew weary. It had been a long day, which began early on the East Coast and included the discomfort of a long flight and too much time in the car. And now he was being fucked with? He was officially pissed at Spence. Mona, too. He tossed the matches on the bar and turned to leave.

"I'm just having a piss with you, friend," the bartender said as he approached smiling. "Walter," he said, picking up the matchbox and tucking it into the pocket of his white dress shirt. Jack shook his meaty hand. "Wally, where I'm from, is an insult, like if I was to call you a sissy – Walter's the name, all these blokes know it, though some around these parts like to make sport of it from time to time. Know what I mean?"

The men at the bar chuckled.

"Funny," Jack said, deadpan.

"That's what I say," Walter agreed, looking contemptuously over at the drinkers, who went quiet. "Now, I understand you have an appointment with M'lady. Let's get to it then, shall we?"

Jack trailed Walter past the bar, through swinging doors into a dining room of 12 empty tables and three busy ones in the same corner. The light was low and surreal, sepia tinted. The patrons seemed antiquated, as if in costume from another era of high balls and tough talk. There was smoke in the air. Jazz played. Walter said some hellos and kept on, through another swinging door into a smaller room in back, dark, with two tables and two semi-circle booths. She was waiting at the horseshoe booth of buttoned leather banquette in the far corner, under a lone, conical light.

*

Smoke curled from the ashtray as she rose, signaling with her hand for Jack to approach. He stood still, staring, until Walter's thick fingers nudged him along.

"Hello, Jack," Angelica Lightman said, her voice smooth, proper-English inflected, her lashes flitting like butterfly wings. She smiled while shaking his hand, gentle yet firm with her grip. "Thank you for joining me."

She looked just like she did in the movies and photographs: waves of platinum hair, thick and lustrous, as if sealed by an invisible varnish, washing down past the sharp collar-bones and rounded shoulders, open in a white halter top that held a full bosom worn like a continental shelf. The trademark mole swam above the full red lips on a sea of milky skin. She motioned with her sparkling, emerald eyes for him to sit.

And it was then that Jack Flaherty, from the hardscrabble streets of Brockton, Massachusetts, the orphaned son of an Irish electrician and his Italian housewife, a former-college athlete and relatively unknown actor, was sitting across a rounded tabletop, in a secluded backroom somewhere near Los Angeles, from one of the most famous and beautiful women in the world.

"How do you like my T-Shirt?" he asked.

"Lovely," she said, her English-accent exaggerated, her plume-like brows rising in faux-approval.

"I was going to go with the white one, but then I realized black was more formal."

"No, well done," she said, retrieving the cigarette with nimble fingers. "Care for a cocktail?"

"Yep."

Angelica Lightman walked slowly to the small bar across the windowless room, her hips switching in the faint light that came from above their booth. From below the bar, she retrieved two frosted Martini glasses and a large cocktail shaker shimmering with condensation. The shaker jangled with ice and the glasses emitted frozen steam as she turned on the toes on her black pumps, tweaking the calves under the hem of black Capri pants, appearing like a vision through the muted light.

"How do you like this place?" Angelica asked, settling into the booth after leaving the cocktail apparatus on the table.

"I gotta come here more often," Jack chuckled, transferring clear liquor from the shaker into the glasses.

"I thought you might like the motif," she said, smiling coyly.

He looked curiously at her. She blinked. He blinked back.

"Not in here, necessarily," she said, catching on to his confusion. "But out front, on the marquee."

"I have to admit," he began with raised brows of his own, gusting relief out of his nose. "I was a little thrown by all the mystery. I didn't know if I was being messed with, or if I was really here for the reason Spence said, so I didn't take much in beyond that big bartender with the ears."

"Walter," she said.

"Yeah, Walter," Jack nodded, "and, truthfully, until I actually saw you, I wasn't thinking about anything more than finding a new agent."

"Oh, don't do that," she said.

"How come?"

"Because I brought you to him."

"What?"

"Did you even notice of name of where you are, Jack?" She asked with mock-annoyance.

"Blue Roses," he said nodding. "I like that."

"Why?"

"I did *The Glass Menagerie* last year in New York, the Tennessee Williams play, and it's the nickname Jim has for Laura."

"I'm aware."

"Of the play?"

"Of course, but I'm also aware that you were in it."

"How?"

"I saw you."

"What?"

"Have a drink, won't you?" she motioned toward his glass, crystallized ice scalloping around the rim. "And I'll tell you how you got here and what I have in mind for you."

*

"You know what my mother used to say about Martinis?" Jack quipped, his Boston accent coming out as his glass was being filled for the third time.

"Tell me," Angelica smiled, holding the ice back with a finger as the last of the frosty liquid drained into his glass.

"They're like boobs."

"Really," she responded, clasping her hands in front. "How so?"

Jack smirked on one side of his mouth, raised his thick brows and slightly squinted.

"One's not enough," he said coyly, "but three are too many."

The glamorous actress of English descent and California beauty released her hands and leaned back, laughing out loud, an unbridled guffaw that bounced around the room, which left Jack feeling empowered.

They were at that point, two drinks down with one to go, where euphoria settles, like twilight, when the bulk of the day is completed, but enough still lies ahead.

Jack basked in the magic felling that filled him, too content to consider how improbable it was that all his recent good fortune had been the product of serendipity. How could he have known that Angelica Lightman had given up films to travel incognito around country looking for talent to promote from behind the scenes for the production company she had recently launched with Spence. Spence had said one of "his people" had seen Jack perform off-Broadway, as if he had an army of scouts scouring the theaters for talent.

Based solely on Angelica's recommendation, Spence had taken him on as a client, and soon cast him in his first movie gig, a supporting role as the abusive soldier, fresh from Afghanistan, who young, Oscar-winner Mina Garcia eventually kills in a film that finished production last year and was ready for release that month. The paycheck, not monstrous by any means, was more than he'd made to date in his career on stage combined. Jack had also liked making the film, shot mostly on location in Bay Ridge, Brooklyn, and he looked forward to seeing the finished product and the cast at the premiere in a few weeks, though theater was more personally satisfying to him: the tension of performing live with no extra opportunity to get it just right. You go out and do the best with what you got in theater, just like in football.

Angelica had seen a copy of the finished film and assured Jack he was great, though the film's success was in doubt.

"It's all about money," she said knowingly. "If your films make money you get to make more, simple as that."

"Your films make money," Jack mentioned, emboldened by their burgeoning rapport and the pint of iced vodka charging his veins.

"True," she said, nodding carefully. "But I choose not to make them anymore."

"How come?"

"I'll tell you when I know you better," she said, before taking a sip of her cocktail, then checking her watch.

Jack surveyed the situation, and came to a snap decision after polishing off his drink. "You think Walter can get me a cab?"

She followed with her eyes as he stood up, perfect posture and taut arms reaching to the middle of his thighs. She noticed the sickle-shaped scar under his chin.

"Leaving so soon?" she asked sadly.

"Yeah, well, I think my mother was right about the Martini thing, and I haven't eaten anything either, and Spence says he has something for me to do tomorrow, so…"

"You haven't eaten?" she asked like a concerned mother.

"No," he laughed, rubbing his flat stomach, revealing the dark hair that trailed from naval to pants button. "And they don't even feed you on planes anymore."

"So you haven't even had lunch?" she asked while standing, her perfect pelt leveling at Jack's chin. "You must be shit faced!"

Jack curled an eye closed, and nodded sheepishly.

"Come this way."

She looped her arm inside Jack's and marched him through the swinging doors. The place was empty, with all the chairs turned up on the tables. A soft light emanated from the bar area, and a dappled mumbling grew steady as they approached the door.

Walter was there alone watching the TV.

"Walter," Angelica cried. "Would you be a love, and make us a couple patties?"

"Of course, M'lady," he smiled, reaching across the bar to pinch her cheek. "You want chips with that, as well?"

She nodded lasciviously.

"And Roquefort on the bun?" he asked swinging around the bar.

Another nod.

"For him as well?" he asked of Jack who was slumping into a stool, arms and legs breaking loose.

"God, yes," Angie cried. "The poor boy hasn't eaten since breakfast, on the East Coast, no less!"

Walter nodded and marched into the kitchen.

*

They ate at the bar, colossal burgers smothered in veined cheese, with crispy fries on the side, while watching a tape-delayed soccer match with Walter. Jack drank club soda as Angelica sipped a deep red wine with her family name on the label that Walter had poured without asking. The satisfying meat and pungent cheese reminded Jack of childhood, when he was growing rapidly and constantly craving protein.

"You a sporting lad, there Jack?" Walter asked once the color had returned to his face.

"Football," he was able to squeeze from a stuffed mouth.

"Really?" Walter asked, considering Jack's height. "Goalie, was it then?"

"Quarterback," he coughed, choking down a hunk of meat.

Angelica looked on, amused. She had eaten half her burger and a fistful of fries, leaving the rest neatly on the plate, turned towards Walter. She crossed a leg toward Jack and sipped at her wine.

"American football," Walter nodded, assuming Angelica's abandoned half-burger. "I can't figure why they call it that, anyway. Makes no sense whatsoever. What's it have to do with their feet anyway? Except for that Nancy who puts it through the posts every once in a while, and that's all he does, all day. I hope they don't pay him much, that one. Then there's the other guys, these tremendous men with pads. Would you believe it! Over their heads and their shoulders and their Willies. Can't blame them there, but their thighs even! They should call it WallyBall, know what I'mean?"

Jack looked at Walter who leaned back against the liquor shelf, lips flapping as he chewed. A dab of blue cheese gathered in the corner of his mouth. Jack tossed down the wedge of bun remaining, popped a few fries, and chewed slowly, allowing the balance from the food to settle over him. He wiped his mouth with a cloth napkin, then draped it over the remaining fries. The effervescent club soda felt cold and celebratory as it washed down the flavors lingering in his mouth.

"How fast you run a 40, Walter?"

"Come again?"

"The 40," Jack repeated. "40 yards. How fast can you run it?"

"Don't know," the bartender mused, crossing his arms over a barrel chest, looking down over his medicine-ball stomach, and massive thighs. "Four or five minutes, tops."

"And what do you weigh?" Jack asked without laughing at the self-deprecating joke. "About 210?"

"I wish," Walter laughed, patting his paunch. "But back in me playing day, yeah, that's about right."

Angelica lit a cigarette, and exhaled away from the conversation before turning back to it.

"You see, there's guys about that size, 210-220, who run the 40 in 4-1/2, 5 *seconds*, and they're looking to tear someone's head off when they get there, so all those pads you're talking about help slow them down just a little bit, and keep guys like me, who usually don't even see them coming, from coughing too much blood the next day. Now I know you guys like to get together in those little groups, you know where everybody's got their arms around each other."

"Scrums," Walter said.

"Right," Jack said. "And while you're down there, hugging, you probably say some awful things to each other, I'm sure, but just be happy some 300 pound monster isn't going to land between your knee and ankle and send a bone in a direction it's not meant to go."

"So what's your point?" Walter asked, crossing his arms and straightening his spine.

"Stop talking out of your ass or some Nancy like me might put a foot in it."

Walter huffed, looked incredulously at Angelica, who had turned the look at Jack, before leaning his thick arms into the front of the bar.

Jack returned the stare, expressionless, knowing he had 4-5 seconds to consider Walter's response: he had the bar between them and was out of reach, so if he lunged, Jack would trap him behind the head and keep him to the bar with the option of snapping his arm back at the elbow; if he came around the bar, Jack would stand up and assume a defensive position focusing on attacking the solar plexus and Walter's left knee which he listed towards while standing. It seemed unlikely things would get physical, considering the time and place, but Jack kept it in mind while considering Walter's response. The man was clearly outmatched by wit, and was already down quite a bit, so it seemed cutting his losses, after regaining some dignity, especially in front of his apparent boss, would be the best move. Walter leaned further over the bar, letting his shoulders ripple, and hardened his stare before standing back straight and refolding his arms.

"I like this guy," he said with a wry smile to Angelica. "Not a Nancy at all."

"You haven't seen me kick," Jack said, extending his hand.

Walter shook it warmly then pulled a pint glass from the shelf adhered to the mirror. He found Jack in the reflection while pouring an ale from the shining bronze tap. "Want one, lad?"

Jack looked at Angelica who had a wink on her lips. He smiled a little while shaking his head, pulling keys from his pocket and tossing them on the bar.

"Brilliant then," he said, wiping the froth off with a ruler before setting the golden glasses down on the bar, then scooping up the keys. "I'll get you a cab then, right after this pint."

Five pints later for each of the lads, Walter tidied up the bar and hit the lights in the threshold before unlocking the door for their exit into the dark night. Jack motioned for Angie to go first, and he followed as Walter insisted with his head and a hearty pat on the shoulder. The silence of the dark night was betrayed by crackling on the gravel in the parking lot beyond the hedge.

Jack and Angelica waited under the entrance portico as Walter turned keys in the front door. A small blast of light burst from behind the shrubs that lined the walk. Another flash of light followed, before the phenomenon repeated, again and again, all along the hedge. Men began screaming Angelica's name, vying for her attention. They charged down the walk.

Jack covered his eyes in a curled arm, and blinked away the temporary blindness while bracing himself for attack. It felt like an invasion of digital camera and smart phone wielding marauders.

Angelica screamed, "Walter!"

A hand grabbed Jack's trapezium and he turned in position to strike. "It's me, mate!" Walter yelled over the cacophony of shouts as cameras continued to flash. "Get inside!"

Jack followed Angelica, skating on her heels, covering her head as if from hail, towards the open door. He turned before entering and saw Walter corralling a ½ dozen paparazzi and moving them violently away as lights continued to flash. A larger, more antique camera was smashed on the ground, and Jack stared at the victimized photographer, a lanky, boyish-faced man with sweeping bangs, who returned Jack's curious gaze, as the other photographers continued to shoot. Jack was familiar with the idle photographer's face, but he didn't have the luxury, at the moment, of remembering how.

Jack and Angelica rushed inside and stood still in the dark foyer. He could hear her teeth rattling, her bated breath coming in and out of her nose. The sound of scuffle continued outside until Walter burst through the door and quickly fixed the lock.

"Come on," he said, taking command.

He lead them through the darkened restaurant and into the kitchen. They resembled school children in line: Walter holding Angelica's hand; Angelica holding Jack's.

"Wait," Walter ordered as they faced a door in the back of the kitchen. Light streamed through some ventilation windows below the ceiling, covering the pots and pans hanging from a rack in ghostly light; the room smelled of the burgers and fries recently prepared. Jack could feel the cold tiles below his feet. His heart beat fast and his head was spinning. Angelica let go of his hand. Walter gently slipped the large bolt from the door and peered outside.

"Come," he said, leading them into the cool and dark night, an orchestra of insects filling the darkened distance with sound. They crossed a small clearing littered with kitchen detritus. Behind a dumpster was an antique Range Rover. Walter opened the back door.

"Get in."

He closed the door gently and slipped around the front of vehicle, where he climbed in the driver's seat and gently started the engine. He put the car in gear and crept along a makeshift and bumpy track with the lights off until entering the parking lot from the hidden lane. Paparazzi huddled along the hedge, their attention on the front door, until Walter hit the lights of his vehicle and stomped the gas pedal, fishtailing through the gravel at breakneck speed.

He jerked down his window and screamed "Yippi-Ki-Yay, motherfuckers!" as the antique Range Rover barreled past the pack of photographers, many of whom leaped into the hedge to avoid being hit.

As they rushed through the pines, Angelica turned to Jack and wrinkled a wry smile. "He's rather fond of the *Die Hard* films."

"You don't say?" Jack retorted before Walter skidded to a stop, checked for traffic in either direction then joined the access road where he accelerated into the empty night.

*

Spence's voice exploded through the phone. "Jesus, Jack! What the hell happened last night?!?"

"What?" Jack grumbled, looking around his twisted sheets in the king-sized bed at the Beverly Hilton. The phone had been ringing all morning. He'd been slightly aware of the interruptions but unable to function until now. Jet lag and alcohol and excitement and concern had eventually slipped him into a deep sleep after settling into his room late last night. Even with the deep fatigue, he had a hard time falling to sleep, consumed by the evening's events. Had he actually been on a sort-of-blind date with Angelica Lightman? Was it even a date? Or was it how celebrities did business? God, was she gorgeous. And great company. He couldn't stop thinking about her. What would have happened had they not been ambushed by the paparazzi? Were they going home together? On the silent ride home, he wanted to hold her hand again, like he had during their retreat through the restaurant, but once they had escaped Blue Roses, and she had made her sardonic comment about *Die Hard*, she had turned away to gaze out the window, not speaking until offering a polite yet sad "Good night, then," when they pulled up in front of the Beverly Hilton. Jack assumed he'd never see her again, which he could feel like weight on his shoulders as he went through the motions of a late check in before arriving in his room, where he suddenly realized that his bags were in his car, and his car was still at Blue Roses, his keys, he believed, lying on the bar. These troubling developments extended an exhausting and amazing stretch which had begun on the other side of the country nearly 24 hours before sleep mercifully arrived.

Jack would have slept through the next day had it not been for Spence's incessant phone calls. When he finally answered, he was in no mood to talk. He held the phone away from his ear to mitigate Spence's squawking.

"I'm alone at the office, and the phones are ringing off the hook," he screeched, as if under siege. "Is Mona there? I sent her over there two hours ago!"

There was a hasty knock upon his door.

"She just got here," Jack said.

"Good," Spence said with relief, and then added before hanging up. "Do everything she tells you."

*

Mona took a long look at Jack and shook her head. She stood in the threshold, as if afraid to enter his room. The plush curtains had been fully engaged, and daylight barely lit the fringe of the thick material. Enough light allowed her to recognize the same clothes he wore yesterday, and even their further shabby condition. She wrinkled her nose as a look of disappointment clouded her face.

"Good time last night, Jack?" she asked, annoyance in her tone.

"Ah," Jack said, sheepishly rubbing his arm. "I guess so."

"Well, I'm glad you had fun, mister, but you have obligations, and one of those obligations is in a few hours."

"OK."

"I need you showered and ready to go in about 30 minutes."

"There's sort of a problem."

"And what's that?"

"All of my things, including my car, are still at Blue Roses."

"Jesus, Jack," she sighed. "You have nothing else with you? Nothing clean?"

He shook his head. "Not even toiletries."

Mona's shoulders slumped and she made the face of a peeved adolescent as she stared vacantly down the hallway. Her silence inspired an explanation from Jack.

"I went there, like you told me, and everything went fine, until later, when we kind of had to escape."

Mona turned on him with another stern glare.

"I know Jack," she said. "It's all over the papers."

"It is?"

"Yes, Jack. It's the talk of the town. This is how we got you today's appointment."

She looked at Jack as if expecting an impressed reaction. None came. He was wondering what the fuck "talk of the town" implied.

"Take a shower," Mona ordered, back in command mode. She looked him over, processing his size. "I'm going shopping. Back in a jiff. We *will* get you there on time."

"Get me where?"

"The Bernie Golden show."

*

When Mona returned Jack sat silently in an arm chair next to the windows by the parted curtains. He wore a terry cloth hotel bathrobe that absorbed shower water from his clean body. The hot water and steam had lifted some of the veil that clouded his head, though he was still somewhat groggy and ambivalent about this supposed coup of a guest appearance. The radio show he had caught a bit of yesterday was ridiculous. People couldn't possibly take it seriously, but Mona and Spence seemed to be in a tizzy. Jack pondered the Angelica Lightman connection when Mona's incessant knock returned to his door.

She handed him two paper shopping bags and a plastic pharmacy sack.

"I'll be downstairs in the lobby," she said. "Come down as soon as you can."

She walked away, and Jack sensed something domineering and manipulative about Mona, something sort of desperate, too, but he dashed all other thoughts as he put his new toiletries to use then tried on his new ensemble: tan Dickies, a plaid, hipster short sleeve with rhinestone buttons, and a linen newsboy hat, fresh socks and cotton briefs.

It all fit, and Jack felt sharp as his boots clicked through the hotel lobby to where Mona sat near the entrance. "Very nice, Jack," she said, with an approving nod to one side of her head. "Now follow me."

She took him by the inside of his long arm and led him outside.

In the hotel's valet area, Mona bypassed the line of tourists and shoved Jack into a cab, handing the valet a wad of cash and the driver another wad, telling him the name of the studio and to keep the change before slamming the door behind Jack as he crawled inside. Mona smiled and waved as the cab drove away, repeatedly opening and closing her hand. "Good luck," she mouthed as the cab exited onto the sun-swept boulevard.

The sunlight poured into the cab, reflecting off the passing cars and metal buildings. The lurching ride heightened Jack's fatigue as he clutched the door handle and waited for respites of shade provided by the palm trees that lined the boulevard. He felt poisoned from the excess of alcohol yet buoyed by the bizarre circumstances since arriving in LA one day ago. He had to remind himself that he was on his way to a radio interview, though the reality of it did not truly occur to Jack until the cab pulled up in front of an enormous shiny edifice on W. Victory Boulevard in Burbank.

He walked across the shimmering sidewalk through revolving doors into the over-air conditioned reception area with vaulted ceilings, marble floors studded with benjamin ficus trees in huge pots, and walls of austere dark tint. The foyer was empty except for armed security, all young and Asian, in starched uniforms who stood erect in pairs on either side of the entrance and elevator banks.

Behind a reception kiosk, beneath a giant metal-sculpted logo, was a prim Chinese woman who spoke in a friendly yet robotic fashion.

"Good Afternoon," she said. "Welcome to Ramcin International. How may I help you?"

Her smile seemed frozen as she waited for Jack to respond.

"Um," he said. "I have an appointment. My name is Jack Flaherty."

The receptionist swiped at a screen that Jack couldn't see.

"I'm sorry," she said, her expression not showing any sorrow, "but your name does not appear in the system. Who is your appointment with?"

"Ah, I'm scheduled to appear on the Bernie Golden Show." For some reason, shame sprinkled Jack's face; he began to rub the back of his neck.

"Ah," the receptionist said. "I see."

She pushed a button and leaned towards a pencil mic to speak very quickly in Chinese. She then pressed a finger to the cartilage along her inner ear and appeared to listen.

She said into the small mic before turning her attention back to Jack. "Please have a seat for a moment." She motioned towards a lounge area canopied by the fikus trees. Jack sat in a guest chair with padded arms beside a glass table piled with magazines he didn't read. With hands on knees, he closed his eyes and breathed through his nose, focusing on his breath. Thirty minutes later the receptionist touched his shoulder lightly.

"So sorry to keep you waiting, Mr. Flaherty. Security will show you up to 30th floor now. You may not visit any other floor. OK?"

Jack nodded.

"When the door opens," she continued, "go to the welcome area and sit. Someone will be with you shortly."

Jack nodded and followed the two security guards who flanked him on either side. In the silent elevator ride, Jack noticed they had matching star tattoos behind their right ears, which he assumed was a moniker from their dojo. The entire environment, formal and foreign, almost threatening, didn't feel like good old back-slapping Hollywood to Jack. And it certainly didn't jibe with the bombastic and crude vibe he got from his brief exposure to the Bernie Golden Show. He thought of the "Get Down with the G-Man" billboard and couldn't imagine that event taking place within these authoritarian walls.

The elevator came to a smooth stop. The doors opened, but the security duo didn't move. Jack stepped off and turned around. He put his hands at his sides and bowed just as the doors closed.

The carpeted landing on the 30th floor was empty. The dimmed overhead lights and cool air created a serene atmosphere. Two hallways jutted from either end of the far wall from where a flat screen hung in front of an L-shaped suede couch that cornered a glass table. Jack sat down.

The sleek black walls were lined with framed fines from the FCC, advertising campaigns, magazine articles, newspaper stories, all dedicated to the Bernie Golden Show. The flat screen looped highlights, including a clip from a celebrity news program that mimicked the motif of network news, regarding the stunt that apparently had made Bernie Golden famous:

"According to eyewitnesses," a suit-adorned and coiffed anchorman reported *"LA based shock-jock Bernie Golden actually did perform on-air fellatio to the adult film star, Amber Jones, who was visiting their studio that day. The FCC is currently investigating this extraordinary event."*

Jack resumed his meditation. After a few minutes, he became aware of a man's voice. He opened his eyes to the sight of an open hand, attached to the long arm extended from a compact, pear-shaped torso over short legs, creating a frog-like figure.

"Jack Flaherty?" the intrusive voice asked. "Jack Flaherty?"

Jack shook the hand that belonged to a short man with long limbs. Under unkempt hair, he wore thick, round glasses held high on a Roman nose. In his jeans, sneakers, and a vintage concert T with three-quarter sleeves, he appeared like a middle-aged lackey.

"Nice to meet ya," the strange man said in a fast, east coast accent. "I'm Jerry DeLaBomba, the show's producer. People call me Jerry D." He spoke like a guy who grew up in New York or New Jersey.

Jack stood up, a full head higher than the odd man in front of him.

"Sit. Sit. Sit. Sit," Jerry insisted. Jack sat and looked up at a still-standing, fast-talking producer. "Sorry to leave you waiting here, but this is a corporate operation, and this whole thing is last minute, by their standards, and I had to personally go upstairs to get you cleared by the Chinks."

Jerry D smiled at Jack, fraternally.

"Who?" Jack asked.

"The Chinks," Jerry said, slightly baffled. "The Chinese that own that own this corporation. The whole top floor is filled with executives and lawyers. A bunch of stuffed suits with bad haircuts, Honk Kong Fuey accents." Jerry made a point of slanting his eyes.

Jack didn't respond.

"What? You don't read the trades? You don't know about these guys?"

"What guys?"

"Ramcin International," he said.

"Rancid?" Jack asked, half-joking. "The band?"

"Ramcin," Jerry said emphasizing the last syllable. "They got a different name over in the Orient, but this is what their branding geniuses back in Beijing came up with for operations here in the west. Ramcin," he said again. "Stands for Radio, Magazines, and Cinema. They own this radio station and dozens of other satellite stations around the country, along with movie studios, TV channels, PR firms, talent agencies, newspapers, entertainment publications. The whole works."

"Sounds like a conflict of interest," Jack said.

"No shit?" Jerry said with sarcasm before straightening his face. "But they paid a lot for that last election. Know what I'm sayin'?"

"No."

"Elections have consequences. Am I right?"

Jack didn't answer.

"Well, anyway, I had a hard time getting you cleared to appear on the show. Turns out the movie you're in wasn't made by one of Ramcin's studios. It was made by some independent outfit, and the Chinks rarely promote things out of house, but when Mona November, called..."

"You know Mona?"

"Of course. I was the AD on a B-film she did back in the day, but that was a lifetime ago, but we stayed in touch, of course, and I was happy to try to accommodate her request, though I needed help from the big guy to get the Chinks to, you know, acquiesce."

"Who's the big guy?"

Jerry D looked dumbfounded at first and then perturbed as he flailed a long arm towards the flat screen. "Bernie. Of course."

Jack looked at the screen, then back at the producer.

"OK," Jerry said, "We don't have much time to go over this, cause of the delays," Jerry said quickly, leading Jack down the carpeted hallway.

"I gotta confess, I'm not familiar with your work," Jerry continued, past closed and solid oak doors, "but Mona sent over an e-file with all your info, a bio and dailies from the film, which I forwarded over to the group to catch up on while we they waited, and they'll be asking you some questions – OK?"

"OK."

Jerry stopped them before a door with a light above it lit red, next to a large glass window that allowed a view of the studio.

"Now, I don't know what you've heard about the show, but this group is top-notch, real pros – OK?"

"OK."

"They're live right now, and when the break comes, we get two minutes, and I'll bring you in and introduce you around, then we get started – OK?"

"OK."

Jack looked through the window into the minimal and bright room. On a long folding table on the adjacent wall, lay a breakfast spread well-picked-over. Beyond the wall to the right was a small room, crammed with equipment and people, visible through it's own window. In front of the window was a long table adorned with two microphones and two tablets in front of two men in headphones who sat and jabbered among the detritus of their unfinished plates, scattered newspapers and magazines. In the middle of the room was another table with two mics and a solitary figure in a blue Dodgers cap and cardigan sweater, legs crossed in an office chair, studying his tablet. An empty chair was to his left. At the head of the room, dead center, on a small stage surrounded by plexiglass, a red-headed man on an elaborate throne/toilet, below a mounted boar's head and a cross bow, engaged the two men in back in animated conversation. Jack couldn't hear a word being said, though it was clear the conversation took place over the head of the man in the middle.

Jack squinted, easily placing the characters he was introduced to yesterday via his car radio. He wondered, for a moment, if anyone he knew would be listening. The red light went off.

"OK, baby," Jerry D said quickly. "Let's get in there."

He opened the door with a card key, and held it open for Jack from inside.

"OK ladies," Jerry yelled over the erupting banter, most of it from the back where shenanigans continued. "Here's our first guest for today, Jack Flaherty, he's an actor starring alongside what's her face, Garcia, in a new movie called *The Killing Kind*, his file's been on your tablet all morning, along with a clip of the film. If you haven't already, read them real quick. We go live in about 90 seconds."

Jerry D pointed his long arm towards the two men in the back. "That's MC Smoov and Sid Fortunato. You know them, of course? They had the #1 sports talk show in nation for years until Sid got the gout and Smoov had to go into hiding for a while cause of some gambling debts."

The big one had meaty hands latched in front, and forefingers forming a fat steeple above the table, gold hanging from one wrist and under the open neck of a golf shirt that stretched to contain his shoulders and paunch. Jack pinned him for a former lineman, a down position guy of some sort from the previous century. To his right, in front of what appeared to be a soundboard, was a mosquito of a Latino in a satin sweat-suit, slouched in his chair, neck protruding, baseball hat turned to the side over a young-but-old gold-toothed face.

Jack nodded, and the two men nodded back before returning to their own conversation.

"And there," Jerry continued, "there in the middle, is the glue of this program, Lenny Temple. You know Lenny Temple, right? The guests sit with him. Go ahead."

Jack approached the empty chair next to a man with a weathered face and a yoga glow, slim in skinny jeans and cardigan sweater over a vintage T. Many-ringed fingers removed a worn Dodgers cap and pushed a swath of golden hair behind a pierced ear with no jewelry.

"Well, well," the man purred. "What do we have here?"

"Uh-oh," big Sid mocked. "Looks like Lenny's in love."

"Who said anything about love?" he responded. "Besides, I like men who look like boys, and this is a man who looks like a man."

Without standing, he shook Jack's hand with exaggerated femininity.

"Hello, Jack Flaherty," he said. "I'm Leonard Temple. Welcome to the so-called show."

"Thanks," Jack said, confirming the voice he recognized from its chastisement yesterday.

Leonard tapped the tablet on the desk in front of him. "I watched some of the dailies," he said nodding. "Fabulous."

"Thank you," Jack said.

"We'll talk more on the air," Leonard nodded, and went back to the tablet.

Jack looked to the front of the room where Bernie Golden sat staring straight ahead from the throne, bright light reflecting off the plexiglass barrier. Jack waited but no introduction to the show's namesake was made. Jack caught Jerry's eye and got a thumb's up, as if the room was in the throes of professionalism. *Real pros,* he thought to himself. *Sure thing.*

"OK, people," Jerry shouted. "We go live in 10, 9, 8, 7, 6, 5, 4, 3, 2, 1..."

"We are our back," Leonard sang into his microphone. "I'm Leonard Temple and you're listening to the Bernie Golden show on FM 101 KBAL in Los Angeles. Along with the regular cabal crew of big Sid Fortunato and MC Smoov, we have with us a newbie actor named Jack Flaherty, who appears alongside Oscar-winner Mina Garcia in the upcoming film The Killing Kind. Thanks for joining us, Jack."

"Ah, thanks for having me," Jack said, leaning too close to his microphone. His adrenaline began to pump, like the first time he set foot on the field in front of a crowded stadium or his inaugural appearance on the stage.

"In this film you play an abusive boyfriend and combat veteran who brings the character played by Ms. Garcia to the breaking point. I saw some of the clips, unlike my pathetic counterparts here who arrive only in time to stuff their faces and inflate their fart toys, and can honestly say the film, and your performance in particular, seems remarkable."

"Thank you," Jack said, still leaning too close to the mic.

Jerry got his attention, and motioned for him to sit back up, leaving a few inches between his mouth and the microphone. Jack nodded.

"There was a real menacing quality to the character, and I'm wondering how you brought that to the role so effectively?"

"Did you fuck her?" A strange voice whispered from the area behind him.

Jack turned to look, and there was no indication of guilt, only those two knuckleheads trying to assume serious faces.

"Yeah, well," Jack began to answer the question, "the character was allusive at first, it wasn't clear that he was suffering from the war, so it was important to try and get across his nature through silence and demeanor even before his violent side, you know, came out."

"How did she taste?" Another whispered interruption came.

"And how did you do that?" Leonard asked, glaring incredulously at the table behind him. Jack noticed the huge smile on Bernie Golden's face as he sat back on his throne.

"Silence can be a pretty powerful tool," Jack said, trying to ignore the distraction, assuming it was some in-house nonsense, oblivious to the audience. "Also, the way the character carried himself I thought was important."

"And how'd you do that?" Leonard queried, maintaining his professionalism.

"Besides the shaved head and 1000 yard stare, I also portrayed the character as lefty, and had him walk with a slight shift to the left with his shoulders, which was easy since I'm a lefty, and there is this subtle connotation with lefties, that they're, you know, sinister or something."

"La sinistra!" Leonard interjected.

"Right," Jack nodded. "You speak Italian?"

"I did some Latin in high school," Leonard said.

The big voice from behind, that of Sid Fortunato, entered the conversation. "Ah, correction, Lenny. You mean you did some Latins in high school."

"Well, that too, yes," Leonard responded with playful nonchalance.

"Not me, mang!" Smoov chimed in.

"Stop lying, Smoov," Leonard teased. "You know we had a thing."

"The fuck out of here," Smoov responded and emphatically waived off the suggestion.

Jack got a sense of the rapport among the personalities, but was wondering why the show's namesake was so silent. Bernie Golden stared at Jack with contempt. He was an ugly man, in a rodeo shirt, mid-30s, with a rust-colored pompadour and a pock-marked face the color of veal. His lips were narrow and chapped. He barred his sharp, mackerel teeth at Jack, and a flash of contempt went through his squinted eyes. Jerry motioned with his hand frantically for someone to end the silence.

Leonard, who had taken notice of the staring contest between Jack and Bernie, stammered, trying to recall where their conversation left off as big Sid perused the bio.

"It says here," Sid began. "You played football at USC. How come I don't remember you?"

"I don't know," Jack answered.

"Well, I guess what I'm saying is that if you were any good, I'd remember you."

Jack turned to study the man. "I don't remember you either," he said, settling back into his chair, arms crossed.

"Hmm," Sid huffed. "How about you, Smoov. You know this guy?"

"Yeah, mang," he said, tapping the table with a long finger. "I think I do know this dude." He looked at Jack. "You a lefty, right?"

"Right," Jack said.

"He just said that," Leonard interjected.

"You played quarterback, like not that long ago. Right?"

"Right."

"You came in like a freshmen or something," Smoov said snapping, "and brought the Trojans back against the Bruins, kept them from going to the Rose Bowl and shit."

"Yeah," Jack confirmed.

"You cost me a lot of money, Esse."

"Sorry to hear that," Jack said disingenuously.

"Well bravo, Jack," Leonard said. "Now that we've established your athletic bonafides, let's get back to the film."

"OK."

"What a minute. Wait a minute. Wait a minute," Sid insisted. "Nothing happened after that? You didn't play no more or what, you got cut or something?"

"I quit," Jack said.

"Just like that?" Sid asked with doubt. "Up and quit after bringing SC back against the Bruins. No one does that."

There was more to it than that, but Jack didn't want to get into the details of it with these morons.

"That's right," he said. "Just like that."

"I call bullshit," Sid mocked. "Smoov, look up this guy on your thingy there."

Smoov was already busy searching through his tablet.

Jack and Leonard exchanged furtive glances in the silence.

"I got nothing," Smoov said.

"Give me that," Sid insisted. "Let me have a..."

The conversation stopped when Bernie Golden took a long, deep, snot-riddled inhale directly into his microphone.

"Do you know why you're here?" Bernie asked Jack after a pause.

"Talk about a movie."

Jack thought maybe the host was going to direct them back to, what he assumed, was a normal conversation and the reason for his presence in the studio.

"What movie?"

"'The Killing Kind with Mina Garcia."

"There is no movie, OK," Bernie stated, agitation on the rise. The back of the room responded to this transgression through various avoidance exercises: crossed arms, chins-on-chest, eyes-on-floor. Leonard shook his head and slowly removed his headphones in a defeated gesture.

"Really?" Jack asked, amused, his Boston accent emerging slightly. "I could'a swore I worked on that film."

"Wrong, you impudent punk!" Bernie raged in a rising voice. "There is no movie because I say there is no movie – alright!"

"Does that mean I don't have to come back out here for the premiere?" Jack asked. "Because it's way more absurd in LA than it used to be."

"You're God-damn right, you don't!" Bernie screamed, standing up behind his plexiglass protected throne.

"This is outrageous," Leonard declared, smacking the table with his palm. "I can't work like this."

"Shut up fag-boy," Bernie spat and pointed at Leonard.

"Come on, boss," Sid said diplomatically. "I thought we were going to try and keep the FCC off our backs for a while?"

"Do you hear me swearing, you fat fucking Guin-bag? Do you, grease ball?"

Smoov produced the sound of a cash register from the sound panel in front of him. Sid pulled off his headphones and pushed back from the table. Jerry D cringed, hands clasped behind his head. *Some pros*, thought Jack again.

"So what am I here for then?" Jack asked the silent room.

Bernie glared at Jack with a flush face and burning ears. "You…are…here…to...talk...a...bout...HER!"

He held up a copy of a daily LA rag with a picture of Jack and Angelica on their way out of Blue Roses. It was from the opening salvo of shots with both facing forward, oblivious to the fireworks about to ignite. Jack looked at the photo and felt a wave of disgust and curiosity wash over him.

"What about her?" Jack asked, wishing for a longer look at the photo.

"Everything," Bernie seethed. "What she tastes like, smells like, how she moans, claws, barks, bites. Everything!"

"Sorry," Jack confessed without regret. "Even if I did know those things, which I don't, it'd be none of ya' fucking business."

The cash register dinged.

"At least admit to me that you fucked her," Bernie begged in a sickening tone.

The cash register dinged again.

"Get bent," Jack spat. "You pathetic fucking loser."

"Make sure I get an invite to the FCC Holiday party this year," Leonard piped sardonically into his microphone. "I think we just paid for the catering."

"Ah, your mother's a whore," Bernie declared with a dismissive wave towards Jack. "Get this loser out of here before I tear him apart."

Jack was over the table with a one-hand spring, and crossing the room towards Bernie Golden's throne with a lot of malice.

"Go to commercial!" Jerry D barked towards the control room. "Cut the mikes!"

*

Richard Evans had been sitting on an ugly and uncomfortable couch for two hours. His ass itched and his knees were sore from crossing and uncrossing. He had reported on time, as insisted in the predawn call he was expecting. "Major" Sincoff wanted to see him right away, and everybody knew why.

There was silence in the copy room when he arrived, early morning editors and reporters hunched in cubicles or crowded in conference rooms going over potential story lines and photographs, sorting the yellow bullshit to peddle that day. The room smelled of coffee and body odor, from the all night shift pulled by people who had no better career options and nothing better to do.

Richard hated this place. This so-called newsroom. He walked under the dim light feigning indifference to the stares that an outfielder might suffer after dropping a crucial fly ball. He wiped the ash-colored hair that swung above his pale eyes and sat down on the couch-of-shame in the alcove in front of the Major's closed door, his delicate fingers stretched on the knees of pleated khakis, the tail of a powder blue oxford draped over his lap.

He had been there an hour already and suffered the glare of every passing employee, but still he waited. The Major himself had passed twice, coming and going from his office without acknowledging him, though on the most recent return he did fart on his way by, leaving Richard alone in the putrid haze.

How did it come to this? Sitting in the egg-like aroma of another man's ass, waiting for his own ass to be handed to him for losing a camera, his own, after being sent out in the middle of the night to take pictures of a couple of actors? This is not why he came to LA from Fresno. He still lived in the same apartment he had when he graduated from USC, which was a cool place for a student, then a Bachelor of Arts candidate with a passion for photography, but not all these years later with nothing to show except a growing exhibit on his walls that nobody sees. The current students and recent grads in his complex stop talking when he passes the pool that Richard is too ashamed to even use anymore.

The Major's door eventually opened, and Richard ventured the threshold looking for a sign of invitation from the mound of man returning to hi desk. The Major was in the familiar colorless suit with wrinkled backside and dashed jacket. The white dress shirt was crumpled along the back and the sleeves were rolled up tight on the elbows. He sat down at his desk and looked up at Richard with the horseshoe of a hairline surrounding the bald, liver-spotted pate, the bloated face and blubbery lips that resembled Hitchcock having been found drowned at the bottom of the ocean.

"Explain," the Major ordered, biting into a fried pastry.

"Explain what, sir?" Richard asked meekly.

"This," he said, digging food from his back molars with a fat finger, motioning with his free hand to the various rags spread across his desk. The Major inspected the gem found by his probing finger and quickly put it back into his mouth.

Richard stepped forward and studied all of the covers with shots of Angelica Lightman and Jack Flaherty, except the one in the middle with a picture of an overweight actress braving a beach.

"The bodyguard broke my camera, sir," Richard said, stepping back behind the chair stationed in front of the desk.

"Did he shatter the card?"

"Um, no."

"Then what happened to the snaps before then?"

"I hadn't taken any yet."

"Why in the fuck not?" the Major asked, glaze gathering in the corner of his mouth as his voice began to rise. "All these pictures were taken before that buffoon broke my camera, which will be taken from your pay, so how come you have none?"

"It was my camera, sir."

"What?"

"It was my camera. It's all I had at home when they called."

"I don't give a rat's ass whose camera it was!" The Major screamed, pounding his desk, making his ½ eaten pastry bounce and coffee to swirl over the rim of a cardboard cup. "I want to know why we don't have any pictures of that god damn couple when we had a photographer at the scene!"

Spit and glaze from the Major's mouth almost reached where Richard stood, and he was happy he hadn't been offered a seat.

"Um, well, the light was bad, and I was lining up a shot using the gas light, which I was about to take when all the other bulbs went off, and then that asshole from Tuna pushed me out of the way, and by the time I got up and refocused the camera was being pulled from my hands by the bodyguard."

"You're an artist, aren't you?" The Major asked with bitterness on his tongue.

"Excuse me?"

"I hired you because you claimed to be an artist – said you could get better pictures than the rest."

"Haven't I?" Richard asked, prepared to run down the list of his exclusive photos that had graced the cover of *Sellebrity Skin,* a place where he was ashamed to work but had little choice as a desperate artist in LA.

"I hate art," the Major interrupted. "It has no place in our society as far as I'm concerned, no fucking place at all. I've worked in this business for 40 years and I know that it's all just shit, shit for the people to fill their worthless lives. Movies, music, whatever – it's all shit. There's no meaning or importance to it at all, except for guys like me who make a living off peddling this crap, and I've got an ugly wife and an ugly daughter who need the money I make to be happy, and you're trying to screw that up trying to make art?"

"No, sir…"

"Listen, I don't give a crap about you, and I'd fire you right now if I could. Shove that shitty contract up your ass while I'm at it, but I've shit-canned too many people this week already, but if I don't see something exceptional out of you very soon you'll be on the street faster than an actress off the bus from Bumfuck. Understand?"

Richard hated getting fired. He had left the photography shop he worked in for years after a dispute with the boss over pay. He had, since then, bounced from job to job for two years, each position requiring a name tag and a disposition he didn't have. The conversation was too familiar: *Richard, can I see you in my office for a moment?* After which he would be thanked for showing up on time and not stealing, but directed towards a career that didn't involve working with people. It was these times he thought about killing himself or even worse: going back to Fresno.

His parents were old and indifferent. He didn't even go home for the holidays any more. He had no friends in LA. Lonely and poor, he took photos all around Los Angeles and kept himself engaged with himself and his hobby while waiting for serendipity. Richard took the job at

Sellebrity Skin because it paid and had a freelancer's contract. He also convinced himself that taking quality photos, even for a disreputable source of the most shallow and yellow journalism, would somehow lead to that break or at least keep him afloat until serendipity arrived. What he knew now, in the fog of Major Sincoff's funk, was that he didn't have the means to quit and he wasn't being fired, so he acknowledged the threat and left, with one last defeat delivered on his way out.

"And don't forget I'm taking the cost of that camera out of your pay!"

*

The light on Jack's bedside phone was flashing when he lurched into his hotel room. There was a pile of Beverly Hilton-monogrammed messages under foot: Call Mona November immediately! He let the notes float to the ground while moving to unplug the phone.

He stretched on the bed cover, arms behind his head, sweat rings staining the underarms of his new hipster shirt. He'd lost his newsboy cap in the scuffle with Bernie and Sid and Smoov. When Jack left the wrecked studio, security guards met Jack outside the elevator banks. They bowed and motioned towards the open car, which he took in silence to the lobby. To his surprise, no one was waiting to accost him there, so he abandoned his plans for both fight and flight, and walked all the way back to the hotel from Ramcin Headquarters at a steady clip, three miles in the mid-day sun.

The effort at reflection, supine on his bed in a luxury hotel, had failed to wash away the ambivalence he felt over the altercation. There was a pervasive sense of guilt about failing so horrifically to promote the movie, potential looming legal matters, as well, but his thoughts began settling more and more on his response to the harassment, especially the quip about his mother. *Fuck them guys...*he said over and over, conviction building each time. Jack's mother had died of cancer while he was in college. It was why he quit playing football. Any disparaging reference to her would be met with extreme prejudice. No exceptions. There was an officious knock on the door, and Jack went to answer it without delay.

"Ah, hello Mr. Flaherty," a young bellhop said, a short-stack of new notes in his raised hand. "Sorry to disturb you, sir."

"No problem," Jack said. "What's going on?"

"Well, sir, I have these messages for you," he said handing them over.

"Thanks," Jack said, taking the messages and moving from the door. .

"Sir," the bellhop said quickly, before the door could shut. "There's something else."

Jack pulled back the door. "What's that?" he asked.

"There's a woman out front who asked me to come get you."

"What woman?"

"I don't know, sir, but she's in a gray car, looks like a rental."

"Four door?"

"Yes, sir."

"Consider me checked out," Jack said, dropping the notes behind him as he walked down the hallway.

He passed through the lobby, feeling some paranoia about being watched, though business transpired as usual among the marbled opulence. A different bellhop nodded and started the rotation of the swinging door in step with Jack's approach. The sunshine was crippling, but Jack had no problem identifying Angelica Lightman, even with the big shades and a scarf over her head, behind the wheel of his rental car, leaning towards the open passenger's window, waiving him over. He let a car pass in the other direction, then crossed over and leaned down toward the window.

"That's some valet service," he said.

"Get in," she instructed.

"Where we going?"

"The airport."

*

"Thank you, Andrew," Angelica said, watching her champagne glass get refilled by the uniformed attendant while comfortably cruising at 25,000 feet.

"Yeah, thanks Andrew," Jack added, taking a sip from his already filled glass. "Again."

"You're welcome, sir," he answered, topping off Jack's glass, before swaying through the carpeted and mahogany cabin.

"I think he likes you," Angie leaned over to inform Jack with a whisper.

"I think you're right," Jack whispered back, looking to the small area in the rear of the private plane where Andrew sat on a stool between the galley and the bathroom.   "Good thing I was able to get that shower and into some fresh clothes before takeoff," he said, tugging on a crisp white T. "I might'a scared him off."

They clinked glasses and leaned back into the wide, leather seats. Jack sat up, and looked through one of the port holes that lined the side of the plane, cloud cover whizzing by overhead with the beige desert below. "Is this thing going faster than a normal plane, or is just me?"

"Actually," Angie answered, "we're going a little slower than a commercial jet, due to our size, but it seems faster because we're closer to the ground and have more things to gauge our speed by."

"Interesting," Jack answered, looking away from his lovely travel partner, no longer in disguise, wearing a sleeveless blue blouse and designer jeans. "So how long will it take to get to Boston?" he asked.

"Six hours, instead of five, approximately, depending on wind, weather, and some other variables, but all in all, it's not a bad way to fly," Angie said, reaching for her leather purse on the small glass table in front of them. "And you can smoke!"

"Expensive habit," Jack mentioned, nodding at her cigarettes in hand.

"I'll say," she laughed, lighting up. "Twenty dollars for the pack, then the cost of the plane, not to mention the fuel. Just awful."

"At least the champagne's included," Jack shrugged.

"Well, that does make it worth it then, doesn't it?" She smiled then clinked his glass again.

They sat in the echo of engine roar for a few minutes, Angie smoking her cigarette and Jack trying to reconcile his bizarre trip to Los Angeles. His exultation over being wooed by one of the world's most intriguing and beautiful women was belied by a lingering sense of regret regarding his behavior at the studio.

"So, on a scale of 1 – 10," he asked Angie. "How bad I fuck up?"

"Oh, I'd say it was about an 11," Angie answered, platinum curls dangling across her upper chest as she bobbed her head in consideration. "Perhaps 12."

"Super," Jack mumbled, rubbing his skull. "So, what's that Golden guy got against you anyway? Unrequited love or something?"

"Hardly," Angie scoffed. "I've never met the man. Not even once. I know nothing of him whatsoever. His obsession with me is really rather a mystery, and I normally like mysteries, but this one I don't care for at all."

Jack pulled his face and considered the consequences of his actions, knowing the woman sitting next to him just judged his screw up as an 11 or 12 on a scale of 1-10. And she didn't even know half of what went down, though she would soon enough.

*

The car service dropped them off in front of a limestone-faced 4-story mansion on Commonwealth Avenue. Dusk was approaching, making the fading light twinkle violet under the sapphire sky.

"Wow," Angie said. "What a lovely home. I adore urban architecture in the east."

The mall between the two-lane traffic was lush green with wooden benches interspersed along a paved path and tulip beds at each corner. The block itself was immaculate; bluestone sidewalks with thick, leafy trees throwing shadows on the historic buildings in the last remnants of daylight.

"Don't be too impressed," Jack warned, fishing for his keys on their way up the wide, sandstone steps "It ain't mine, and I'm not exactly on the top floor."

He held open the heavy wooden door, holding both their bags in the other hand, and slid in behind Angelica to open the second door, a lighter, glass-plated divider separating the foyer. They entered onto the main hall, black and white marbled floor, wood-framed artwork hung evenly on the rouge colored wall above the stained wainscoting. A grand, mahogany stairwell curved slightly up to the second floor.

"I love it," Angie declared, holding the carved end of the railing, standing on the first step, looking up. "I just love it. You never see places this…regal in Los Angeles."

She began to climb the stairs.

"That's great," Jack said as he remained on the landing. "But don't start calling Architectural Digest just yet." He continued down the hall of the entry level.

"Where are you going?" Angie asked, leaning over the railing.

"This way," he said, pointing down steps directly under the stairwell.

"Oh," Angie said. "What's down there?"

"It used to be an apartment for the Super," Jack said, taking the steep stairwell into darkness, "but they don't have one anymore, so they started renting it out about five years ago at a wicked low price."

Angie descended the steps and looked down, reluctantly at Jack's descent. "Who are 'they'?"

"Some old Blue Bloods. Bought the whole building and kicked all the tenants out. They leave for South America the day after the Sox get eliminated from playoff contention every year. They'll be back by opening day in the spring."

"Really?"

"Really."

"How wonderfully eccentric."

"Yeah," Jack quipped. "Rich people kill me."

"And what's your purpose?"

"I take care of the place when they're gone. And when they're here."

At the bottom of the stairwell, Jack hit a switch, and fluorescent light from a low ceiling illuminated the area.

"You coming?" he asked Angie, still on top of the stairs.

"Of course," she said, creasing a smile. She took the stairs slowly in her heels, avoiding the railing on either side.

"The best thing about this place," Jack said while working the key, "is that if you're in a hurry to get to the bathroom, once you open the door you're practically there."

He pushed open the metal door, and the entire apartment, bathroom and all, was nearly at their fingertips. Jack walked in and dropped the bags at the foot of a mattress on the floor and went straight to the bathroom in back, adjacent to the alcove for the kitchen with a shallow sink and a hot plate on the counter above a mini-fridge. Angie tried to ignore the sound of urine splashing while looking at the décor of light orange sponge impressions on the plaster walls. Above the unmade bed was a large Basquiat canvas that Angie studied, thinking it might actually be an original. She opened a closet door on the wall leading to the bath; there was a neat stack of T-shirts and jeans, brown and black boots on the ground in military order, a pair of running shoes, and a few dress shirts hanging next to a garment bag.

She smiled at the surprising order and dignity of the space, when something caught her eye between the crumple of sheets spilling off the bed and the waist-high bookshelves that portioned that area from the rest of the studio. Angie picked up the large white bra that lie next to the mattress and let it dangle between her thumb and forefinger.

"Make yourself at home," Jack said, startling her from behind.

She dropped the bra, and spun around. "It's not mine. I found it right there."

"It's not mine, either," he said, with feigned defiance.

"Well, then, to whom does it belong?" Angie retorted, hands on hips, mock-indignant at such a discovery.

Jack looked around the room, settled his eyes on the guitar case, the unmade bed, and the dishes in the sink. "Nancy Jean."

"And who is this Nancy Jean?"

"Nancy Jean is Jeannie," he said going to make the bed. "My cousin, she lives in New York now, but she stays here when her band's in town."

"She just shows up?" Angie asked, curiously not dubiously.

"Yeah, she usually tells me she's coming, but she's got her own key, and she's more like a sister, really. There's probably be a message on the phone," Jack added, nodding towards a cordless phone in a stand on the counter.

"You have a home phone?"

"All I got," he said, forgetting about the smartphone from Spence stashed in his suitcase.

Angie noticed the missing "R" in some of his words, and was even more intrigued by the background which inspired this threadbare and antiquated existence. There was no media in sight besides a record player on top of a crate stacked with records.

"So, what shall we do now?" she asked.

"Let's go hear some music."

*

They changed into fresh clothes for Friday night: Jack in a short-sleeve vintage button-up with a pointed collar; white with a pink-stitched crisscross pattern. He wore a faded brown corduroy cap that matched the square-toe boots with the heel in back covered by the frayed ends of faded jeans. Angie donned ink-blue jeans, flailed at the cuffs over pointy black heels with a white, ribbed sleeveless crew. "I'd left my T-shirt collection back in Los Angeles," she quipped, pulling the shirt from Jack's closet on her way to change. She came out of the bathroom with her hair pony-tailing out the back of the Red Sox cap she found behind the door and a black bra in hand which she stuffed into her small suitcase on the end of the bed.

She touched up her lips to match the color of the hat, and returned the stick to the black leather shoulder bag looped over her arm. "Prepared?" she asked Jack who stood by the door, hands deep into his pockets, diverting his eyes from the savage breasts loose under his soft cotton shirt.

"Only if you are," he said, holding open the door.

*

They hailed a cab as darkness sifted down on the regal Back Bay of Boston, in the early hours of an autumnal New England evening, riding in silence away from the Brownstones and Queen Anne's and mansions towards the row houses of the South End.

"Up here," Jack said, and the cab pulled over in front of a bar with a small bay window, the "Deluxe" pieced on the titled marquee in red plastic letters. There was a smattering of people out front, and Jack followed them in the door leading Angie by the bare arm.

The place was crowded, barely room to stand in the open area in front, next to the unmanned instruments tucked in the left corner by the window, under overhead lights. A worn bar took up the far left side of the back room, with barmaids teeming behind it to fill the orders of the mixed-hipster/South Boston crowd seated along its nicked expanse, or piled three deep behind them, their muted conversations rising towards the tin ceiling. They mixed comfortably, casual in their status on the fringe of culture. Tattoos on the tail bone and/or shoulders of most of the women, displayed by tank tops with black bra straps showing; the men in plain T-shirts, tats on their forearms or biceps, hair and face in need of shampoo and razors.

Crowd-piercing waitresses balanced trays while negotiating the ravaged wooden floor of the front room or filling orders at the station on the near end of the bar. The walls throughout were brick with dangling mirrors and a dart board right over the head of where Jack and Angie settled in the nook on the far wall where the front room ended.

"Hi ya, Jack," a petite waitress with black spaghetti straps over her pale vegan-body greeted him with an Irish accent. "And where have you been?" she asked, her black eyes up towards his.

"Galloway, Mary, looking for you."

"Feckin' liar," she said, stomping lightly on his foot. "What can I get you then?"

"Two Rocks, please," he smirked, feigning pain.

Mary looked at Angie, gave her the once over, and then brought her eyes back to Jack.

"This is my friend, Angie," he said informally. "Angie, this is Mary Minihane.

"Hello, Mary Minihane," Angie said, smiling and extending her hand.

"I don't know what you heard, Lassie," Mary said, leaving Angie's hand empty, "but if you think there's going to be a wet T-shirt contest here tonight you're sadly mistaken."

Angie crept the hand back, along with her smile, staring down Mary for a second before looking at Jack. "Feckin' liar," she said, and stomped his foot, not so lightly.

"Hey," Jack yelped.

"Good one, Lass," Mary said nodding. "I'll be back with your beers then."

"What are you smiling about?" Jack asked Angie, once Mary disappeared into the crowd.

"You didn't find that humorous?" she asked innocently.

"Actually, I did, but you've been smiling since we got here."

"I have?" she asked, looking around the bar, the chatter and faces surrounding them.

"Yeah, you have," Jack said with a friendly suspicion. "What's up?"

"I'm just having fun," she nodded, and went back to watching the room.

Angie absorbed the crowd with great interest. She took in the scene as if it were air. The proximity to people was stimulating, especially considering the anonymity under which it transpired. The lack of bra, as expected, kept eyes off her face, allowing her to observe from the under the visor of the cap something she deeply admired – people at play, going about their business in pedestrian fashion. She'd been traveling incognito for years, almost always alone and at a distance from those she observed. She longed, often, to be one of them; tonight, she was.

Mary appeared through the fog of bodies, her tray lined with beers.

"I got you four, just to keep you happy for a while. This place is a zoo now, isn't it?"

"Thanks," Jack said, handing two bottles to Angie, then replacing the two he took for himself with a $20.

"Would you be expecting change?" Mary asked.

"Would it matter if I was?"

"No," she said brashly. "Next rounds on me, though."

"Thank you, love," Angie said.

"You're welcome," Mary responded with resignation. "I'll be back to check on you soon enough, in the meantime, Sláinte."

Jack and Angie clinked green necks and began drinking cold beer in the warm room.

*

The boisterousness of the bar settled when a young woman entered with two men and another woman all about her age. Besides the eyes suddenly set on them and their modest smiles, they were distinguished by an extra cut of cool, a layer of skin deeper on the onion everyone in the room was trying to peel, indicated by their sense of purpose and style which smacked of concerted effortlessness.

"Wow," the raven-haired woman said into the lone microphone, tossing her already mussed locks, pulling down the black belly-shirt that revealed more belly than shirt. Her skin was pale compared to the midnight-hair, and pitted in a few spots high on her rounded cheeks. She had a gap between her upper front teeth that was on display when she smiled and said with a feigned airiness, "OMG. Thanks, for, like, coming!"

"That's Jeannie," Jack leaned towards Angie's ear to whisper.

The room quieted, even in back by the bar, as the male guitarist and female bassist, flanking Jeannie on respective sides, forming a V, made final adjustments to their instruments while the drummer on a three piece-kit sat back against the wall on a padded stool, bohemian hair and trimmed beard, sticks spinning like pinwheels around his long fingers. Jeannie strapped on an acoustic Yamaha with a daisy on the strap, confirmed it in-tune with an E chord, played with a slow drag over shiny strings.

"You know," she mused into the microphone. "I love small gigs. You come, set up your gear, get a bite to eat, come back and play. None of that bullshit soundboard shit at the bigger spots, where they never seem to get it right. Was anybody at The Roxy last night?"

A few people in back grumbled, and a stocky guy with wide shoulders and a crew cut, strangling a beer bottle beside the makeshift stage, yelled. "That was fucking bullshit!"

"Wow," Jeannie responded, stepping back playfully from the intensity and proximity of the comment. She turned to face the band. "Should I tell them about it?"

"No," the guitarist retorted quickly, finishing the finagling with his amp and standing up, sheared hair and face stubble matching the black Gibson electric slung over shoulders covered in a blue T-shirt with "Romney 2012" in crinkled white type.

"Yo," the bulky crew-cut asked with indignation. "You voted for Mittens?"

The sardonic guitarist smirked among the smattering of cruel laughter from those in the crowd who were hip to irony.

"No," the guitarist explained. "It's a joke."

The man looked around angrily with shame coloring his face and informing his body language.

"Are you a soldier?" Jeannie kindly asked the man.

"Yeah," he said.

"How long have you been home?"

"Not long."

"Thank you for your service," she said.

The man smirked and then smiled, appearing handsome and intense. Jeannie could feel his pain as she dragged E chord and began singing slowly, softly in sync with the guitar strum. The voice was angelic, round and full of soul, singing the song of a tortured soul. The drums shuffled lightly behind while strings on the bass were picked a single note at a time. The electric guitar kicked in, adding tension and urgency to the drawled chords. The rhythm picked up and Jeannie's voice climbed an octave for a bridge that led into a howled chorus. The electric guitar bent a double note straight towards the ceiling and back down as cymbals crashed and the chorus repeated before settling into the mild opening tempo, and Jeannie sang softly again.

Angie bobbed her head slowly, absorbed in the words of the swaying chanteuse, whispering in amber through another verse. Jack stood still, choked, as always, by the poetry and power of his dear cousin, waiting for the explosive bridge that gives rise to the song's rancor. A maelstrom of orchestrated combat among the band ensued, with Jeannie cranking on her acoustic, a string breaking and flailing around her as she pounded out chords over the piercing triad of electric notes repeated by the guitarist, hunched over his instrument, his head rising slowly on the off-beat, eyes closed tightly. The slender bassist with long black hair bobbed her lowered head as her cohort in rhythm systematically smashed cymbals and pounded skins, until the floor fell out and everything became very quiet for the song's heartbreaking conclusion.

Silence.

"Yeah!" Jack called, shattering the stillness.

The rest of the room joined in praise with claps and calls.

"Woooao!" Angie yelped, holding herself like a parishioner under a revival tent. Heads turned towards the corner where they stood, including Jeannie who had just handed over her guitar to the lead guitarist to replace the busted string.

"Well, well," she said into the microphone with a sly smile. "It looks like cousin Jack's home early, and he's been a bad boy."

The band members smirked with conspiracy, though the rest of the room failed to react.

"Come on," Jeannie playfully pleaded to the crowd. "Don't you watch the TMZ Channel? What's wrong with you people?" Jeannie shook her head in mock disappointment. Jack knew his cousin – an artist in every true sense of the word – loved her celebrity smack. The magnitude of channels and magazines dedicated to contemporary celebrity fodder were his little cousin's guilty pleasures. It's no surprise she knew of yesterday's debacle in the studio, but he didn't want it discussed, and he didn't want any attention, considering his clandestine company. He made this clear with a stare that served as a statement between family.

Jeannie smiled at Jack while taking the guitar back and strapping it over her shoulder. "Never mind then," she said, her fingers shifting into an open chord position on the guitar neck. "Looks like cousin Jack has a date. Let's do a happy song for him – OK guys?"

Two quick snare strikes set off an up-tempo number with the electric guitar leading the charge, chords jack-hammered while Jeannie strummed quickly and the rhythm bounced and rolled along through the verse and chorus of a rocker.

Angie squeezed Jack's wrist, immersed in the happy, head-bobbing, shoulder-swinging crowd who had abandoned their hipster veneer to the joy of music. She looked around at the room of bright eyes and lost herself in the glow.

No one noticed when the handsome and damaged soldier slipped out of the room.

*

At the end of the 60-minute set, where Jack and Angie had grown closer, physically (occasionally bumping hips, nudging shoulders, clinking beer bottles) and spiritually (glances of communion), they whooped, whistled, cheered, and clapped with the rest of the overjoyed crowd. A half-circle of adoration formed around the stage as Jack, with his head above the crowd, caught his cousin's eye and signaled the Italian gesture for a good meal, by turning a finger into his cheek. Jeannie gave a great big nod and gap-toothed smile before returning to her admirers. Jack and Angie parted the crowd for the comfort of the cool night.

"OK," Angie gushed, lighting up a cigarette. "That was brilliant!"

"Yeah," Jack said as they walked along the busy avenue under street lights, alongside the onomatopoeia of cars whooshing past. "They've been really good pretty much since the day they got together."

"Jesus," she said hugging herself. "I feel like a teenager, you know, without all the neuroses and pimples, of course."

"Don't tell me you had pimples," Jack said, happy to have an excuse to nudge her again. It had been 20 minutes since they last touched and he was anxious for the feel of her skin on his elbow.

"Well, not really," she said, letting out a foggy cloud towards the sky. "No neurosis either, not until I was older, at least."

"What would you have to be neurotic about?" Jack asked. "Couldn't imagine."

"Me neither," she said, sidling up playfully at the corner as they waited for the light to change.

Jack put his hands deep into his pockets and waited in the stillness as the pedestrian crossing signal displayed an orange hand. Angie smoked and basked in the warm machinery of night. People were out on an electric Friday evening; couples in various stages of familiarity, ranging from anxious first-date distance to newly-in-love canoodling with hands in motion, to been-in-love routines of separate smartphone focus. Clusters of college kids passed, looking for love or adventure in the twilight of another semester. Young hustlers and toughs from Boston's ramshackle neighborhoods walked briskly into the secrets of their silent nights. Cars hurried by, windows open, music mixing in a cacophony above Jack and Angie who stood motionless on a street corner, surrounded by the blurry lights and pulsing sounds.

"Where are we off to anyway?" Angie asked when they had the light, crossing the street in tandem.

"We're gonna meet Jeannie and the band at her father's restaurant."

"Lovely," Angie said, going with the flow. "Though I do hope it's close."

"It's in the Italian section, the North End, which is a pretty good hike from here – we can take a cab if you want, but we have some time to kill so I figured we'd walk a bit."

"Care to trade shoes?" Angie asked, stopping to display a heel on bent leg.

"Yeah," Jack nodded. "Sorry about that. I'll get us a cab."

"No, no," Angie interrupted his gaze down the boulevard. "I like the idea of walking. Let's just take our time, can we?" She slipped her arm inside his.

"We can," Jack said, coveting the feel of her fingers on his skin as they headed north on Columbus Avenue.

*

The night smelled like apples, and they walked the whole way without much conversation. The only dialogue was Jack pointing out historic sites as they skirted along the lower side of the Boston Common and passed Beacon Hill and Faneuil Hall, closing in on the harbor and its brackish breezes.

Once beyond the expressway, they arrived in front of the restaurant in the North End on a brick street lined with places to eat. "Da Giulio" was scripted in white across the red flag out front and on the matching awning. They entered just as a van loaded with instruments parked in the alley alongside the restaurant in a spot marked "No Parking" in spray paint.

Inside, Jack greeted the staff with kisses on both cheeks and hugs. They were all in black pants with black vests over white dress shirts. Roughly half the tables were occupied. The rest looked like they had recently been. Jack introduced "Angie" to the staff then led her by the arm across opaque tiled floors and white plaster walls as the dappled light reflected off framed mirrors.

"Where are we going?" she asked.

"What? You think Blue Roses is the only restaurant with a secret room?"

She laughed as they left behind the staff who cleared and reset open tables while the remaining dinners chimed away with their silverware and conversation.

Jack ducked his head into the kitchen to yell "Salve" before continuing down the narrow corridor, past the bathrooms, then turning under an archway into a brick-walled room with a long table and a metal door on the other end that the band was entering through.

Angie grabbed Jack's wrist. "I think I'll use the loo, to clean up a bit before meeting everyone," she said. "Is that all-right?"

"Of course," Jack said, turning back towards the archway. "Right over there."

"Thanks," she said, kissing him on the cheek. "Be back in a bit."

"Yeah," he said, watching her walk away, heels turning on the tiles. "In a bit."

His trance was broken by a push to his lower ribs.

"Snap out of it, cuz," Jeannie said, smirking, beside him.

"Hey," he yelled and tucked his cousin under his long arm, kissing the top of her head. "Great gig, kiddo."

"Thanks," she said, hunching with exaggerated meekness and a firm grin. "We rock."

"Yeah!" the two men from the band roared from the spots they had assumed around the table, flashing hand signs of the devil into the air and banged their heads.

"You couldn't ditch them?" Jack asked Jeannie, looking right at the guys.

The guitarist gave him the finger while the drummer bowed. Jack waived to the meek bassist. She smiled and looked at her hands.

"Sorry," Jeannie said, joining her band. *"The band that eats together*…does something together."

"Keep working on that one," Jack advised. "Have a seat, and I'll take care of the food. I'll find your father while I'm at it."

Through the hallway, he hit the swinging kitchen doors and raised his hands in reverie to greet his friends and occasional coworkers.

*

The small plates on the end of the table were covered with the scraped skin of artichoke leaves. The heart of the vegetable was on a platter, listing to one side, among the detritus of squeezed lemon wedges, bread crumbs and oil. Another platter, formerly layered with golden eggplant, was dotted with flaked fry coating and smudges of tomato sauce and oil. Long glasses were filled with effervescent liquid. Two bottles of prosecco filled an ice bucket beside Jack at the far end of room. He looked at the empty seat across from him, the full glass of prosecco sparkling softly. Angie had yet to return from her trip to the bathroom. When Jack went to check on her, she was out front gesticulating into her cell phone, where she stayed throughout the first course that was devoured in silence.

"What happened to your date?" Jeannie asked.

"She's out front," Jack said, sizing up his cousin's inquisition. "On the phone."

Jeannie wiped her mouth slowly with a cloth napkin. "I see. Did you bring her back from LA, you know, like a souvenir?"

"Something like that," Jack said.

The boys in the band adjusted their positions to enjoy the unfolding repartee between cousins. Jeannie took a slow sip of prosecco.

"And how was your trip?" Jeannie broached to Jack. She held a blink for two beats too long.

"Not bad," he said, leaning back into his chair, crossing his long arms.

They guys guffawed, while Jack stared at his cousin, devoid of expression. The bassist gnawed at artichoke leaves.

"That's one way to describe it," Jeannie said, a smile leaking towards the side of her mouth. "From what I understand, you got caught carousing with Angelica Lightman, and then busted up Bernie Golden's studio over the whole thing."

"Spare us the silent treatment on this one," Bobby, the guitarist, begged. "If you ever were in the same building as that chic, I gotta know about it."

Jeannie said, "Apparently Bobby here had quite a thing for her when he was in high school."

"Yeah, I had a poster of her in front of my bed," Bobby said, "and a sock beneath the bed so stiff you could fend off a prowler with it."

"Oh, gross!" Jeannie squealed.

Everyone laughed.

"Sorry I'm late," Angie interrupted, tossing her hat on the table and taking a deep sip of prosecco. "By the way," she said to Bobby after removing the glass from her lips, shaking her hair so that it unfolded along the back of her shoulders. "I'm flattered."

Jack smiled while the band looked stunned; Bobby, in particular – his jaw wide open, hands out to the sides as his seat tipped involuntarily back.

*

The commotion surrounding the sticky sock revelation had died down after sufficient ribbing. They went back to it occasionally for fun, but the conversation had progressed and the players in the room had digested the presence of a celebrity with a predicate of cool. The boys and the reticent bassist sat at the far end and had a subdued conversation while Angie and Jeannie bonded across from each other at the near side. Jack was in the kitchen working on the second course.

"So, tell me about the band," Angie prompted Jeannie.

"The band," Jeannie said pragmatically. "What can I say? We've been together since graduating."

"From where?"

"Austin and I went to The New England Conservatory. Bobby and Lauren were at Berklee."

"Impressive," Angie said, looking down at the trained musicians, then back at Jeannie.

"Not to A&R guys apparently, because we're still trying to get signed five years later." Jeanie finished a swig of sparkling wine, and pulled the bottle from the bucket. She filled Angie's glass before her own.

"Thank you," Angie said with a sweet, buzzed smile. "Surely there must be interest. You guys are fantastic."

"Sure, there's always been interest," Jeannie said smirking, the alcohol manipulating her emotions. "Since the very beginning. We're really, really good. We can play and write songs, but there's always something."

"I don't understand."

"I don't either," Jeannie said leaning into the table, crossing her arms under her heavy chest. "These guys don't want to talk about it, and none of those A&R guys come right out and say this, but I think if I lost 20 pounds, maybe got my teeth fixed, we'd been on our third album by now, heading towards a greatest hits collection."

"Cut the shit, Jeannie," Bobby warned. The others agreed with their annoyed eyes and sour faces.

"Come on," Jeannie begged. "You think they would have kicked us off-stage last night if I was a size 4?"

"Who kicked you off stage?" Angie asked, offended.

"It was incredible," Jeannie said, shaking her head. "There's like a handful of bands playing at the Roxy, which is a pretty big gig for us, so we tell everyone we know., and we get there way before hand to set up and be professional, but the show is late getting started, of course, because they can't get the sound system right, and every band is pushed back further and further, and we're second to last so we end up going on way late, but we didn't complain, and we, like, just finished our third song or something, and this asshole that runs the venue, whose fault it is that nothing is on time in the first place, comes out on stage and whispers in my ear that we get one more songs because the headliner, this Adrianna McCoy chic, has to go on on time because, you know, she's the headliner and there are people from her record company there, and blah, blah blah, and at first, I'm like, 'Oh, OK,' me being all me and all, and then, I start to get pissed. I'm thinking about all the people we contacted about coming, and a lot of them showed up, and we took off work and drove up from New York, which is like $100 each way in gas for the van, and these guys had to find places to crash, so I'm like, 'No way, man,' and we play a song and go right into another one, and at the end of the second one the guy comes out again and starts waiving his hands in the air saying our set is over, but I count down and we start up another song, and we're playing like our fastest song, and the guys are thrashing and jumping around, and I'm banging my head, and we look like Spinal Tap or something, and this guy starts signaling with his hands, you know, like cutting his throat, to the sound guy, who cuts off the fucking sound! Can you believe it?"

"And what did you do?" Angie asked from the edge of her seat.

"I don't know," Jeannie said, slumping.

"Oh, you should have seen it," Bobby said. "It was so punk-rock. She kicked her mic stand into the crowd, and people from, I assume, the record company or something, started yelling up at us, and they're starting to fight with some of our fans, and the asshole stage manager guy tries to grab Jeannie's arm, and Lauren pushed him from behind into the crowd."

Angelica looked at slender, reserved Lauren with raised brows. She returned a tight smile and a naughty nod.

"So," Bobby continued, "luckily all the drums and amps were provided by the house, so we just packed up guitars and got the hell out of there."

"It was so crazy," Jeannie said solemnly. "I'm sure any A&R guys there weren't going to ask for our CD after that."

"So, why don't you just do it then?" Angie asked her.

"Do what?"

"Loose the 20 pounds and get your teeth fixed."

"Come on," Bobby questioned Angie. "What are you doing?"

His protective response, to the woman of his teenage fantasies no less, was brave and telling. Jeannie was clearly beloved by her family and band mates.

"No, no," Angie said with a raised hand. "It's a legitimate question. I'm just curious, if you think that's the only thing holding you back from your dream, why don't you just do it?"

"I don't know," Jeannie said pensively. "I really thought a lot about it, but I guess my feeling is…is that I wouldn't be me anymore, and the music would suffer for it."

"I see," Angie said. "What a great answer."

"I mean," Jeannie continued. "Do you think anyone would have asked Patti Smith to get a boob job or Aretha Franklin to have her tummy tucked or stapled or whatever? No way. This is who I am, and I'm not changing that for anyone. I don't care what they're selling these days."

"Allora," Jack said entering with a bottle of red wine stuffed into each of his front pants pockets, holding a platter of thick spaghetti coated in a sheen of tomato sauce, smelling of onions, bacon, basil, and grated cheese. "Bucatini alla' Amatriciana."

"And," Jeannie said affirmatively to Angie, "I'm not giving up food . I'd rather starve...or something like that."

The pasta was portioned out, a moderate nest of noodles on each plate. Grated cheese was passed and sprinkled before fork tines were twirled and bites were concluded with slurps. From around the table, moans of pleasure came from licked lips; and Angie gave Jack a sinful smile. He stood to fill the oblong glasses with a ruby-red Chianti Classico, pouring over each diner's right shoulder. The room was filled with the song of food music: scratched tines on ceramic; mono-syllabic approval; the brush of a napkin across lips; swallowed wine: repeat.

The alley door abruptly opened. "What are you doing in my restaurant?" a large man with a round face bellowed. His thick Roman accent and his gesticulations – shaking hands out to each side – made him even bigger than his formidable size.

"Hi, Daddy," Jeannie said, wiping her mouth, returning to her plate.

Cries of "Guilio" came from the boys in the band and Lauren's face lit up with a smile. Jack stood, threw his hands up in welcome to his Uncle. With curious eyes, Angie studies the overwhelming yet gentle man.

"All this 'Guilio,' 'Guilio' I hear, but no one answers," he said with feigned seriousness, the thick gold bracelet on his wrist, and the medallion between his unbuttoned collar, bouncing with pinched fingers. "We don't allow musicians here. It is bad for the business."

The band laughed and continued to eat.

"They laugh," he says, coming around the table, stopping behind Angie, resting a hand on her shoulder. "But what do they know about business?"

"Where you been?" Jack asked. "Romero says you went out an hour ago."

"What Romero?" he asks with a frown, matting down his fair comb-over. "What does he care where I go?"

"He cares, Uncle Guilio, and so do I."

"How come? How come you care where I go? It's a free country, America."

"I know that Uncle Guilio, but you used to never leave the restaurant during hours, and Romero says you've been disappearing a lot lately."

"Don't worry," the man shrugged his shoulders and face. "It was slow, very slow this evening, so I go to take an espresso with D'Angelo, talk affari."

"Business with D'Angelo?" Jack asked. "He's the competition."

"What, competition? This is not calcio or war. It is business. We have the same things in mind, so I talk sometimes with the other padrone. I am not a stubborn man."

Jeanne scoffed, *pretending* to choke on a sip of wine.

Her father ignored the slight and addressed his nephew. "Don't worry," he said. "I know what I'm doing."

"Everybody in the kitchen is nervous, Uncle Guilio."

"Why?" he asked. "What are they nervous about?"

"Because, they're not stupid," Jack answered with respect. "Things have been slow and then you start disappearing. They know if you sell to D'Angelo, he's gonna bring in his own people."

"Ah," Guilio cut off the conversation with a raised hand. "Basta, Nipoto," he declared, then looks down at Angelica. "Dimme, Bella – how was your Bucatini?"

"Fantastico."

"Brava," rolled from Guilio's tongue, his green eyes twinkling. "You know some Italian?"

"Well, sort of," Angie answered with quiet confidence. "My father is English, so, growing up, I spent a lot of time in Tuscany."

"Of course," Guilio purred. "The English, they love Italy, and if you ever go to England, you know the reason. There are so many inglese in Toscana now, they call the area between Firenze and Siena, Chiantishire."

"Bravo," Angie said with the pinched-finger gesture.

Guilio smiled, dimples caving into his pillow-like cheeks. "Who is this?" he asked the table. "This woman of Chiantishire?"

"A friend," Jack answered.

"Whose friend?"

"My friend," he said.

"Good," Guilio said with a big nod. "It is good to have friends. I thought that maybe if you were friend of my daughter, maybe you could teach her the Italian."

"Daddy!" Jeanne interjected.

"I know, bimba," he said. "You too busy with music to bother about my language." He planted a kiss in his palm and blew it across the table to his daughter. "You know," he said, touching Angie's shoulder again. "My daughter is trained to sing in the Opera!"

"I know," Angie says. "She's amazing."

"You heard her sing tonight?"

"Yes."

"You know, she gets her singing from me."

Jeanne returned the blown kiss to her father, staring at him with a warm smile.

"It is true," he said. "Later, maybe, I will sing some Puccini for you, but now, we must eat."

*

After a long course of Guilio's specialty, a whole chicken broken down and roasted with a sauce of lemon, garlic and oregano, washed down with an assertive Brunello di Montalcino, Angie slipped into the alley for a cigarette and a phone call.

She returned as the band lingered over bowls of gelato.

"Hey," Jeannie declared with a smile. "Nice shirt."

"Isn't it?" Angie asked, flattening the stomach of the t-shirt with the band's name "Jezebel" scribbled across her ample breast with red lip-stick.

"You couldn't have sketched our faces on there?" Bobby asked.

"So sorry, Mr. Bobby," Angie teased, hands on hips. "I hope I haven't ruined your sock contribution for the night."

As the room howled at Bobby's expense, Guilio asked, repeatedly, under the clamor, "What sock? What is this sock about?"

"Trust me, Daddy," Jeannie said, through her wild laughter. "You don't want to know."

"OK," Guilio said, his hands gesturing up in a small chop of acceptance.

After order was restored, the meal's momentum had ceased. It was time for the evening to end. The staff had been sent home, so everyone helped clear the plates into the kitchen where Jack stood in front of the deep double-basin sink and washed the dishes with a powerful nozzle head, handing them to Angie for drying with a hand towel. Guilio finagled with the cash register as the band, in the back room, wiped the table and mounted the chairs.

The ad hoc restaurant staff gathered in the front room, closing time complete. Goodbyes and thanks were bestowed upon Guilio as Angie drifted towards the blinds-drawn storefront. She peeked through the slats, and returned to provide the evening's benefactor with a warm hug and kisses on each of his tremendous cheeks. "Don't worry," she said. "Business will get better."

"What? Me, worry?" he asked, leading Angie by the arm towards the front door. "Il mundo giro…"

"Yes," Angie nodded. "The world does turn no matter what we do. Doesn't it?"

The door was unlocked and opened, spilling the coterie of artists on to the early-morning sidewalk. Angie shook her hair from under the Red Sox cap just in time for the first camera flash to explode. It was followed by others in a stretch that resembled machine gun fire. "To the van!" Angie ordered as the swarm of photographers encroached on the entourage. Angie remained still, forearms across her eyes, a feigning deer in the headlights of camera's flashing on her in a white t-shirt with a band's name scrawled in lipstick in front, under the awning of a North End restaurant named Da Guilio. Jack peeled back from the retreating group, retrieved Angie by the arm and pulled her into the alley as the band members reenacted Beatlemania, singing "A Hard Day's Night" in the echo of the walled in corridor, as if they were being chased by hordes of fans instead of their new friend being pursued by an aggressive passel of photographers. The flash of the cameras caught them scurrying into the van, screeching down the narrow alley to an exit on a parallel avenue. They continued singing and laughing the whole way home, "It's been a hard day's night."

*

"Wait a minute," Jeannie wondered aloud as the van settled in front of the building on Commonwealth Avenue. "Where am I going to sleep?"

Various offers and alternatives rattled around the inside of the van until Jack ended the debate by yelling over the clamor, "Has anyone heard the weather?"

"What?" Jeannie asked.

"The weather. Does anyone know if it's supposed to rain tonight?"

The van's radio was dialed to an AM station, and they waited 8-minutes for a news cycle to predict a cool and pleasant evening with a low in the high-50s.

"Problem solved," Jack said, opening the side door to the van, climbing out and offering a hand to the two guests of his two room apartment.

After another round of sidewalk-goodbyes, the van rolled away and Jack, Jeannie, and Angelica passed through the grand entrance door, into the foyer, the hallway, and finally the stairs that descended to Jack's basement studio. Leaving the women in the threshold of the open door, he pointed towards the bed while walking past, saying "Jeannie," before turning the corner, fumbling briefly in the closet, and returning with a rectangular box under one arm, blankets and pillows under the other, and a label-less long bottle tucked into his back pocket.

"You come with me," he said to Angie, trudging up the steps with his city-camping gear intact.

"Where are we going?" she asked when they began climbing the decorative stairwell leading up and away from the lobby.

"You're not afraid of heights, are you?"

"Not really, no."

"Good, because we're sleeping on the roof."

"OK," Angie said, her heels clomping in step behind Jack. "Can I help with your things?"

"I got it," he said without pause.

"Well, how about the bottle, at least – I'd hate to have that fall out and break over the stairs."

"OK, Jack said, stopping on a landing between floors.

Angie removed the bottle from his back pocket, pulled the protruding cork, and held the rounded neck of glass to her nose. "Ahhh," she sighed. "Grappa."

"Yeah," Jack said, continuing the climb. "Uncle Giulio smuggled that back from his last trip to Italy."

"Having met the man, I suspect it's rather good."

"We'll see," Jack said, climbing ever higher.

After the top floor of apartment doors, there was a last set of stairs that curled around to a landing with a metal door at the end. Jack flicked back the hook-shaped lock and pulled open the squeaky door. The cool air refreshed the stair-climbers, and their eyes were filled with the glow of a city night. The roof was large and severely sloped on all sides, except for a fenced-in landing dead center, wooden-planked and bound by a waist-high iron fence high above the cornice that framed the outer perimeter of the building. Angie walked to the edge, resting her arms on the railing, looking at the Citgo sign flashing triangular in front of the darkened chasm of Fenway Park. The Prudential Building, the cities only skyscraper, was a turn of the head away, as was the Boston Harbor, the Common, the golden dome of Beacon Hill, and the endless low rooftops interrupted by the hasty flow of the river Charles dappled in moon beans.

"What a pretty town," Angie declared, turning to lean her tailbone into the railing. The full moon was over her shoulder, above Fenway as if it had been spying on the Sox and couldn't stand to leave once the season ended. "And this where you were raised?"

"Well, yeah, sort of," Jack said, sitting Indian-Style on the ground, pulling collapsed vinyl from the box he lugged upstairs. "I grew up in Brockton, which is a city south of here, not too far, but I spent a lot of time in Boston as a kid, especially the North End with my grandmother, in the apartment where my mother and Jeannie's mother grew up."

"Where are they now?" Angie asked, picking up the grappa bottle, and making to pour some into an imaginary glass in her hand.

"Both dead," he said.

"Sorry," she said, studying the label-less bottle.

"Crap," Jack said, sitting up. "Glasses. I'll go down and get some."

"No, no!" Angie insisted. "This will do."

She pulled the cork and took a small, wincing sip. She let the warm liquor course down her throat, settling into her very full belly. "Whoof," she said, shaking her head. "Strong."

"Yeah," Jack said, busy spreading out the crumpled vinyl mass, which he had just hooked up to a black object. "It's a digestive. And a necessary one."

"Agreed," Angie said, taking another small sip before re-corking the bottle and putting it back down on the deck. She fished through her purse, pulled out a cigarette, and lit it with a disposable lighter. "What are you doing there, anyway?" she asked, blowing smoke at Boston stars.

"It's an air-mattress," he said, pushing a switch on the black cylinder, which immediately began humming, causing the vinyl to slowly inflate. "Cool, huh?" he asked, walking towards Angie in long strides, dipping smoothly to pick up the bottle and settle a full head in front and away from her.

"You know," she said, reaching across her stomach to prop the elbow of her smoking arm, which held the cigarette just above her left eye. "I never said I'd sleep with you."

Jack remained still, staring into Angie's tilted green eyes. He uncorked the bottle and took a sip. He walked back to the mattress, and kicked at the stiff folds around the edge. He walked back, and stood in front of her again – closer this time.

"I didn't realize I was being presumptuous."

"You are," she said, flicking her cigarette down the slope and onto the flats of the tar roof.

"Sorry about that," he said, slipping his sinewy forearms around the narrows of her waist, latching his hands in the small of her back.

"You are forgiven," she said, taking his moonlit face in her hands.

*

"We can't do this," Angie declared to the morning sky. The sun had climbed over the harbor and was high enough to impose upon on Jack's closed eyes. Angie was tucked under his arm, sheltered from the intrusive rays. "We can't do this," she repeated, her voice reverberating through his torso, shaking him awake.

"What?" Jack queried, turning his naked body into Angie's. "Can't do what?"

"This," she repeated, flicking her wrist at the sky.

Angie sat up, letting the covers fall from her breasts.

"Ah, I think we already did," Jack suggested, modestly. "A couple of times, if I'm not mistaken."

"Not that," she said, slapping his leg beneath the blanket.

She twisted her torso to face him. Jack studied Angie's face, framed beautifully by matted platinum hair, smudged eye liner buttressing the despair behind green eyes. Her porcelain skin, white as a pealed pear, grew smooth in the settling light across the rooftops.

"I'm so sorry, but I woke up this glorious morning, next to an intriguing and handsome man, expecting photographers to be camped out around us on roof taking our photo."

Jack rubbed the area between her shoulder blades.

"It wasn't always like this, you know," she said, staring straight ahead. "My mother, who was a bigger star than I ever was or will ever be, always said that the key to being a star was knowing how to have a healthy relationship with the media. She would pose for pictures when spotted about, and that was enough. And when she stopped making films, they left her alone. We had a nice quiet life together, living in the hills of California, and I simply went off to school, public school, mind you, like a normal kid, studying acting, doing some films here and there. We would travel anywhere we wanted without concern. But when she got sick, things changed. Those reporters she was frinedly with all along were now pariahs, calling our house non-stop, legions of them camped outside our gate. The doctors could barely get inside without being harassed. Two of them quit. Couldn't stand it. It was so awful, and I'm convinced it – the intrusion – accelerated her illness, and caused her to die faster than she would of, and, I fear, not on her own terms."

"How'd she die?"

"Cervical cancer."

"I'm sorry."

"Me, too. I was so sick about everything that I swore off California, America even, and went back to England to live with my father, but that didn't work out so well."

"How's that?" Jack asked, now sitting up with his arms wrapped around his knees.

"Well, I was 14 or so when I returned, though I had lived there for many years as a child. I came to California with my mother at age 8, after my parents had separated. When Mum passed, I didn't mind returning to England, for it felt a bit like home. And it was so serene. We lived in our own castle in the countryside, my father and I and much of his staff. It was very quiet. Chauffeurs and private school and all that. And then, a few years later, my father talked me into making *Il Bel Paesa*, and this so-called little film he had promised we'd make ended up getting quite a bit of attention."

Jack never saw the film. It came out when he was in high school, where the softcore porn components of it were subject to as much adolescent banter as the artistic aspects that appealed to so many critics. Angelica Lightman played the comely and courageous daughter of an English doctor living in the Tuscan countryside during World War II who has a torrid affair with an older Jew she finds hiding in their barn.

"Oscars for the whole family," Jack joked, circling his hands as if ordering a round of drinks.

"I hate that thing, God," Angie huffed. "It's just some silly object I keep in a closet – it has no meaning to me; though I did masturbate with it once."

"What?"

Angie giggled. "Yeah, well, it is sort of phallic, and recluses do get lonely, you know."

"No wonder actresses get so hysterical when they win – they've just won the world's most prestigious sex toy."

Angie cackled, and her shoulders lowered from where they had been hunched around her neck like a collar. She lay down next to Jack, who took her hand as her face grew somber again. "Well, that aside, the awards were good because they brought me back to Los Angeles for good."

"And why's that?"

"I was furious with my father, even before the awards. I wasn't comfortable with some of the scenes, and he assured me they would be edited out, which they decidedly were not. And then he pulled me out of prep to do publicity nearly half a year. It was exhausting and intrusive. My God. I never wanted that much attention, and suddenly I was this enormous star. A sex symbol, really. I had all these creeps obsessed with me. Some of them still are, like that wanker who urinates on my photo whom you had the pleasure of meeting yesterday. This was something I never asked for or wanted, and, all along, my father acted like the Academy Award didn't matter to him, but when I won for actress, and he for director and producer and whatnot, I knew, I knew he had been holding out on me along, and that I was just his muse, his magnet for attention, just like my mother had been before. Narcissistic asshole."

"I think that's actually 'Sir Narcissistic Asshole,' isn't it?"

Angie laughed, sadly, and curled into Jack's side. "Not yet, though I suspect he's working on that. I was stupid to think that this would work, and I shouldn't have thought to bring this blight upon anyone. It wasn't my intention, I swear. I try to do what I do quietly, privately, but I'm still a human being, and I get so lonely sometimes, and from the first time I saw you on stage I just wanted to meet you. You just seemed so, so comfortable. And I crave comfort. I really do. I didn't know it would lead to this, and you'd be smart to stay away. Last night, though, was so much fun."

"Oscar worthy?"

Angie smacked Jack's leg again. "That was fun, too – really fun, God – but I meant more the being together at the venue, and walking through the city, and having dinner with friends – those are the things I miss most. The intimacy of friendship, I guess."

"Then why'd you call the tabloids?" Jack asked.

"What?" Angie sat up, her face shattered. "Why would you say such a thing?"

"It was slick, I admit," Jack acknowledged. "But it came to me while I was sleeping: you go outside to make a phone call, color your t-shirt, ah, my t-shirt, then a half-hour later the cameras show up? And then I remembered how I had to come back and get you after we all ran away. It seemed a little strange to me, and then I started thinking about the other night in LA, how that was your place so you could have easily arranged for that whole scene. What's the deal?"

"All-right," Angie smirked, her hands up in defense. "I'm cold busted, but it's not like you think. I had nothing to do with what happened at Blue Roses; that's my sanctuary, the only place in LA I can go to, and I wasn't ruining that for anything or anyone. But it started me thinking about how the paparazzi found out, and I had my suspicions, which I wanted to confirm, and as we were sitting there last night listening to how your Uncle's restaurant was struggling, and how your cousin's band was, too – I had this idea: I'd call dear Spencer and tell him where I was, and if the cameras showed up, I'd know who the mole was. And if they were going to come take our picture, might as well make some publicity for your uncle's restaurant and your cousin's band, as well."

Jack crinkled his eyebrows and squinted into Angie's eyes.

"I swear," she said, under the glare of investigation. "I have no other agenda here beyond finding out if I can trust my dear friend. Besides, this is your fault anyway."

"Mine?"

"Yes, handsome – I certainly don't have any films coming out, so the publicity is wasted, unless it can be used it to make news about someone else, so I suspect were both being used here, but you, my dear, are the main attraction."

"No chance."

"Spencer has known about Blue Roses for years. He joins me there for dinner at least once a week, and he has never, ever said a word to anyone. Now he decides to blow it on the night that one of his young clients is in there…with someone who has a bit of notoriety? Come on, it's a promotional masterpiece on his part, I must admit."

"Would Spence really do that?"

"That's what I had to find out, and it seems plausible now. Spencer is a dinosaur, and I have to go out finding clients for him, and you're the first one to actually ever land a decent role, so I think he's working it for all he's got. He links you to me, and, well, an overnight sensation might just be in order."

"That's sad," Jack said, feeling his existence whirl around him. "I thought he was your friend."

"He was like a father to me growing up! Truly. But Hollywood society is his life, and if he stops getting invited to those back-slapping events, he'll be dust. It's as simple as that."

It started to make sense to Jack, this all being part of Spence's plan to make him a star, but it might not have been working out so well, especially after the fiasco with Bernie Golden. "Let's go downstairs," Jack said, rising. "We gotta figure this out."

"Not so fast," Angie creased a coy smile, putting a hand on Jack's bare chest and pushing him down on the mattress. "Like I said, it's lonely being a recluse, and I'm not ready to start dusting off my Oscar just yet."

*

Inside the tiny apartment Jeannie was sitting on the bed with a newspaper opened in front of her. "You gotta see this, Cuz," she said, as Jack and Angie trudged in with the sleeping paraphernalia under his arm. They sidled up on either side of Jeannie and looked at the photo taking up the center of the gossip page of a Boston rag: Angie curled at the hip with shoulders and profile tilted up and away, "Jezebel" scrawled across her lunging breasts; the storefront and flag of Da Guilio in clear view behind her. "Starlet Does Bean-Town" headlined the caption. The paragraph below stated how the reclusive actress Angelica Lightman was spotted outside a North End restaurant, Da Guilio, after dining with her favorite rock band, Jezebel, and her renegade boyfriend, actor Jack Flaherty who had recently trashed the radio studio of LA-based shock jock, Bernie Golden.

"Has your father seen this?"

"Are you kidding? He called my cell phone ten times this morning before I finally got out of bed."

"What he say?"

Jeannie tucked into her chin and tried to do an impression of her father. "This is beautiful. Tonight I will need a red rope outside the ristorante."

Jack raised his brows at Angie, and she returned the gesture with a tight-lipped smile. "Now what?" he asked.

Angie pointed at the paper. "What happened there?" she asked. "It says something about an altercation in the studio? I assumed you simply walked out after the argument, rather gallantly, I imagined. But Spencer was blathering last night about your appearance being a 'fiasco' or something, and I thought he was just being somewhat hysterical, but apparently there's more to it than that, isn't there Jack?"

"Yeah, Cuz," Jeannie piped, rubbing her hands together. "Give us the details. You get medieval on somebody or what?"

Jack took his time making coffee, whipping up some scrambled eggs and toast while recounting the physical details of what went down in the studio after the mics were cut:

Once over the table, he had approached Bernie's perch and bashed the plexiglass with the heel of his black boot, sending pieces of shattered plastic showering across the room, covering Bernie who had fallen back into the corner.

Jerry yelled about getting security and dashed out the door.

Jack heard the table squeal behind him as it was moved, and turned in time as big Sid lumbered towards him, arms wide for a bear hug. Jack spun away from him before sweeping the ankles of the large man, sending him flying into the air, and eventually onto his side in a pile of shards. Sid moaned, but didn't move.

Jack sized up the rest of the frozen room then walked between the separated tables and out the door. The Chinese security detail were not aware of any problems, apparently, or didn't give a shit, so Jack strode with them down the hallway, breathing through his nose, exhaling the adrenaline, and when the elevator bell rang he entered the open doors, bowed to the martial artists, hit the lobby button and glided down the 30 flights. After crossing the lobby unfettered, he went around the rotating door and into the hot Los Angeles afternoon.

"My Goodness," Angie heaved, balancing a plate of eggs on her lap from where she sat on the side of the bed. "No wonder Spencer is so ripe. Pathetic Bernie Golden must be out for blood!"

"Rock on, Jackie boy," Jeannie praised, slapping her cousin a resounding high-five as she passed from the bed to the bathroom.

"I don't understand," Angie squinted from lack of comprehension. "What prompted such violence?"

"He called my dead mother a whore."

"Oh, shit," Jeannie peeped from the bathroom. "I guess they didn't know about all of your black belts."

"You practice karate?" Angie asked.

"Shotokan," Jack said. "It's like karate, but a little more physical."

"Aren't you full of surprises?" Angie said.

"That's about it," Jack shrugged.

"No wonder you weren't frightened by Walter."

"I was frightened by Walter," Jack said. "Believe me. I'm just incapable of taking shit from people."

"Apparently not," Angie agreed, more concerned than impressed. "You could be in real trouble, Jack. Was anybody hurt?"

"I don't know," Jack said with a grimace. He took a sip of coffee, resting a bare foot against the kitchen wall. "I was out of there before anybody got up."

"Whoooh!" Jeannie yelled from behind the bathroom door. She began to sing,

"Everybody was kung-fu fighting."

"Stop encouraging him," Angie shouted towards the bathroom before turning the conversation back to Jack. "This is serious, Jack," Angie persisted. "Maybe you're not in real trouble with the authorities or anything, but if you've truly humiliated those chaps, they can make you pay."

"Those guys are fast as lightening…" Jeannie continued singing from the bathroom.

"How?" Jack asked, concealing the smile inspired by his silly cousin.

"How? By smearing you all day, every day. They have a lot of listeners, and if they can hurt the box office of your movie, make you a less appealing entity, your career could really suffer as a result."

"So?"

"So? You might not give a rip, with your laconic indifference, but other people's livelihoods are involved here."

"Mina Garcia is the only name involved, and she's untouchable."

"No one's untouchable, Jack, not in Hollywood. Besides, it's not just the other actors. It's the director, the crew, not to mention a whole shit load of money that people poured into making that film."

"You think Mina Garcia masturbates with her Oscar?"

"Jack!"

"You masturbate with your Oscar?" Jeannie asked. "You rock!"

"Jack," Angie pleaded. "You must take this seriously."

"OK," he said, washing his coffee cup out in the sink. "What do we do?"

"Come to New York with us," Jeannie screamed. "We have a gig tonight. Can you sing, Angie? Maybe we can get you on stage for some backup or maybe even a duet! And Jack, can you kick somebody's ass, please?"

"You see what this does to people?" Angie asked in a hushed tone.

Jack smiled. "She's just having fun. And besides, you started it."

"No, you started it," she said, coming up to poke him in the chest. "I just added a little fuel to the fire."

"OK, so how do we put it out?"

"I don't know, but, for starters, I think we should get out of Boston."

"Come on. We just got here."

"I'm serious. They will find out where you live and make life hell, for your friends, neighbors, everybody."

"What are they, the CIA or something?"

"Worse. They're celebrity spooks," she said in a feigned officious tone, "and they're bound by no rules, no code of ethics whatsoever."

"Fine," Jack said, retrieving his duffle from the closet. "Where do we go to lay low?"

"New York does sound good," Angie answered, looking towards the bathroom.

"Yes!" Jeannie howled. "You guys are like the coolest couple ever!"

"You hear that?" Jack asked. "I guess we're a couple now."

Angie titled her pretty head and looked pleased. "I guess we are."

*

The van pulled up and the door slid open. Jack and the girls dashed from the entrance of his building into the van. Bobby turned from the driver's seat with dark sunglasses and a Yeshiva-beard hanging crooked across his face. The other two members of the band, in the way-back row, sat staring straight ahead, stone serious, same get-up of beards and glasses.

"Very funny," Jeannie laughed, punching Bobby in the arm as she climbed into shotgun position. Once Jack and Angie were settled in the middle-row, the door was slammed and the van chirped off into the quiet Saturday morning.

They negotiated the labyrinth of Boston streets and hit the highway unmolested. On the Mass Pike the itchy disguises were ditched, and the talk was of the newspaper photo, and what it might mean for the band. Jack and Angie were silent.

On 95-South, Jeannie worked her cellphone as wind and FM radio whipped through the van, traveling steady in the middle lane, Providence passed with New Haven ahead. Angie tucked into herself, resting her head on Jack's shoulder, his arms clamped around the back of the vinyl bench, his legs extended into the front cabin between the bucket seats. Bobby looked down at the crossed brown-boots but didn't say a word.

Jack refused to contribute to the monopoly McDonald's had on the Connecticut stretch of 95 – "a philosophical and gastronomical imperative" – so they exited the highway and ate burgers on a barge docked along the Norwalk River. They sat outside, in sunlight tempered by the river breeze formulated in the nearby ocean, seagulls circling overhead. The smell of salt and oil mingled around them. After lunch, while the van was being refilled at an adjacent gas station, Angie and Jack walked down to the waterside and skipped stones across the placid surface of the river.

"I'd like to stay here a while," she had said, but went to the van without hesitation when they were called for the last leg of their journey to New York.

The van crossed from Queens into Manhattan and began the bumpy ride down the shifting and manic FDR, the East River with its crossings and eddies lining the left side of the drive. At Houston Street the van exited and traveled west through the tenements of the Lower East Side on the wide avenue, its sidewalks teeming with pedestrian traffic. Angie inched her face toward the window and studied the street scene on parade.

Bobby turned the van up 1st Avenue and followed a rush of green traffic lights to an open lot on Seventh Street, where he waved to a big man in a wooden chair, leaning back against a support pole of a cyclone fence. The man rose to unlock the gate. The van was parked in a corner of the gravel and weed lot, the equipment left inside as the occupants exited. "We're playing around the corner tonight," Bobby explained on the sidewalk. "And the owners of the club own this lot, too, and they let bands park here since it's close, and a safe place to keep the equipment." He nodded more towards the 6-foot man than the 12-foot fence.

"Can we leave our bags here for now, as well?" Angie asked.

"Don't worry, lady," The big man grumbled. "We're good."

"Thank you," Angie said and smiled, adjusting the scarf and sunglasses donned before leaving the van. "So, to where are we off?" she asked the group.

"Brooklyn," Lauren said.

"Same," said Jeannie.

"Queens," Bobby said. "For Mamma's cooking."

"Washington Heights," said the drummer.

"None of you live around here?" Angie asked.

They all laughed.

"You can come home with me, if you want," Jeannie said to Angie and Jack. "But, I'm just going to take a nap, maybe make some more phone calls about the gig."

"That's alright," Jack said. "We'll be all-right."

"Are you sure?" Angie questioned, scrunching up what was left of her exposed face. "It will be safe for us to be out in public?"

"Everyone's anonymous here, even you secret agent lady."

"So we'll see you tonight at the gig?" Jeannie asked.

"Yeah," Jack said. "We'll see you later."

"Later."

The road trip was over, and the respective travelers slipped into the fledgling shadows of a late afternoon in Manhattan.

*

Jack and Angie walked to Third Avenue and down to the Bowery, passing without notice on the busy sidewalk where the cafe's had outdoor seating beneath the renovated facades of the Lower East Side face lift from the early 21st century. The streets were crowded and stylish, boutique-lined, an abundance of exclusive items for purchase or consumption. The tattoo of the area's once gritty and complex history, an incubator of art and attitude, had been fully removed.

Across Delancey Street, Jack and Angie entered the lamp shade district and we're soon into Chinatown. They waited on the corner of Canal Street in front of a tiered yellow and red pagoda before crossing the mouth of the Manhattan Bridge into the sidewalk bustle that Jack was a full head above. The sound of clanging kitchens and rancid smells mingled among the banter and bartering of Mandarin and Cantonese tongues. Angie stopped to buy a parasol from a corner-vendor, twirling the rippled red cover as they continued out of the congestion and up a stairwell behind the towering Metropolitan Building.

Across the street, a high wrought-iron fence that separated the sidewalk from the grassy, tree-strewn expanse that led to the back of City Hall – a grand white structure of three very wide floors – was buttressed by concrete barriers, and a roving security detail. The area was open, especially in comparison to the canyons of Chinatown, with a bouncing-cloud sky behind the building tops of lower Manhattan. Jack veered Angie towards the breeze emanating from the expanse of the Brooklyn Bridge.

The entrance to the walkway was concrete, but as they rose in a slight incline, the river below came into view when the wooden planks arrived underfoot, with the magnificent stone coil-suspended arch ahead. Bicyclists rattled the wooden slats, focused on their exercise, as the pedestrians stayed to the right, unanimously silent in the awe overhead and to each side. The East River, wide and welcoming, rippled in golden light past the seaport adorned with masts of model ships that once arrived in the harbor, loaded with goods and passengers from foreign lands. To the other side, the pale blue Manhattan Bridge reflected light as a subway car rattled beside the vehicular traffic. The Williamsburg Bridge was just beyond, regal and elongated across a wide stretch of river.

At a peak of the Brooklyn Bridge, on a landing under one of the stone arches, Jack and Angie stopped. Photographs were snapped incessantly, but the only star present was the staggering testimony to what man was capable of in harmony with nature: the tiny islands in the gaping mouth of the harbor at the end of the Manhattan, islands not developed much beyond their initial use as way-stations for the teeming immigrants who were touching land for the first time in months, a land that held all their dreams and aspirations; the Statue of Liberty off in the distance, corroded by her centuries in America, but still reaching and proud; barges, charters, and sail boats slipped atop the choppy waters in the shadows of a cluster of high-rises that were, in many ways, the center of the universe.

They sat on the expanse and stared in silence as the afternoon passed, then they walked, arm in arm, down the bridge as the sun settled over the glass and steel horizon from the west, filling the slats in between the buildings and along the streets with rose twilight. The light had dissipated in Manhattan, and they sunk back into the shadows of the valley between the bridges, as the tops of buildings and bridges and sky hoarded the white light that hung over the city like a shimmering blanket.

In a ramshackle noodle shop in Chinatown an old woman with a kindly face brought steaming bowls filled with vegetables and shrimp. They sipped the steaming broth from small ladles, picking the solid pieces out with chop sticks. They filled ceramic cups with tea from a pot the old woman brought without a word.

"Had you ordered any of this?" Angie whispered, leaning over the small table they shared beside the front window. It was the first thing either of them had said since leaving the bridge. There was no one else in the small room, except the old lady in her faded frock who stood watching them with nurture, like a grandmother, from behind the wooden counter.

Jack shrugged, and shook his head, creasing a clueless smile. He made eye-contact with the elderly woman, and pointed to the roasted ducks which hung behind her in a mahogany glow. The woman nodded then disappeared to the back.

She returned from the kitchen with a platter of carved brown meat, glistening skin in-tact, garnished with rounds of scallions, thin pancakes, and a bowl full of viscous plum sauce. The platter was laid on the table with a bow before the woman returned to her station behind the counter.

The couple smiled at each other in the glow of anonymous hospitality. They lined the pancakes with duck meat, slathering them with the plum sauce before rolling into crepes. The balance of the savory meat with sweet and salty sauce was perfectly complimented by the cut of meager yet pungent scallion. They slowly worked their way through a ½ dozen pancakes each, steadily awakening their spirits with each bite.

When the platter was cleared and the tea drained, the old lady approached the slumping, satisfied couple with a coy smile and a slip of paper.

"Feel better?" she asked, laying the check, written on a scrap of paper, onto the table before collecting the plates.

"Yes," Angie affirmed, her eyes sparkling appreciatively.

"Absolutely," Jack concurred, reaching for tab.

"Enjoy your life," the old lady demanded with a resolute nod, followed by a quick smile, before vanishing into the kitchen.

Jack left twice the amount of the meager tab on the table, and helped Angie from her seat and into the magic of early evening.

*

Under the faltering sky, Jack and Angie crisscrossed the grid of downtown Manhattan, keeping to the shadows of side streets, stopping quickly for espresso at a cafe' on Bleecker Street, and later a gelato near Union Square, which they spooned while sitting on the small set of steps that faced 14th Street. No one gave them a second look, as if they were just two life forms in the irrepressible parade at the center of the universe on Saturday night.

"Tell me about your family," Angie requested once Jack had returned from depositing their spoon-scrapped cups in a nearby garbage can. "The ones I haven't met." "Let's see," Jack began, draping his wingspan over raised knees, latching his hands in front, looking at the street. "My father was an electrician, Irish, from a little parish in Dorchester, and he met this Italian girl from the North End, standing in the crowd at the Boston Marathon, and they fell in love, got married, moved out to the suburbs, or what they could afford as a suburb, Brockton, which had always been a pretty tough place, but they had a house, at least, and a son. But I don't really remember my father cause he fell down an elevator shaft when I was five."

Angie covered her mouth and gasped, "How awful."

"Yeah, it was. I was a kid, you know, and everybody spoiled me for a while, and I kind of adjusted to the way things were. Uncle Guilio became like my father figure, and I had coaches and a sensei later when I joined the dojo, but my mother, she never really got over it. She hardly left the house except for church every morning. The rest of the time, she sat in there with the blinds closed, watching TV, movies and soap operas and the news. But when 9/11 happencd, she freaked out. Said that footage of the second plane flying into the tower, that they kept playing over and over, made her sick. Said they were traumatizing a whole generation of kids. TV was the real terrorist. Made me get rid of the thing. She quit going to church. She just sort of quit everything."

A pigeon cooed towards Jack's toe, and he shooed it away with is big boot.

"What did you do?"

"I took care of her, I guess. She always liked the movies on TV, so, you know, in my spare time, which there wasn't much of, cause I had school and sports and a job with a landscaper, I went to the movies and then I'd come back and tell her all about it. This was like the only pleasure she had. And I would go, two, three times a week, and I'd tell her all about them. Every detail I could remember so the time would last longer. I'd remember certain lines, too, act the parts out for her."

People passed on foot and bike and skateboard as night sifted down onto Union Square. Angie wrapped her hand on the underside of Jack's arm.

"So this was like your training as an actor."

"Kind of," Jack shrugged. "I even got a part in the school play, hoping it would get my mother out of the house, but she never showed."

The sadness of that moment lingered in the silence.

Angie raised her eyebrows, "Well, as they say in storytelling 101, and then what happened..."

"I played football, and I was good at football, so I got a couple scholarship offers around New England, but there was also one to play out at USC. The coach at my high school was a Brockton guy, but he had gone out west for college, knew some people at SC, and he was really advocating on my behalf, I guess cause of all that had happened in my life. He got me a full ride, but I didn't want to go. All the way out there? California? Nah. Too far from my mother. I was going to to go to UMass out in Amherst. Maybe Boston College or the University of New Hampshire. But my mother said she wanted me to go to Hollywood. Said she wanted me to be in movies. She was getting a little batty around then, from all that time in the house, but she wouldn't let it go. Kept saying she wanted me to go. So I went."

Jack laughed to himself.

"It was kind of working out like she hoped. I auditioned for a few parts, didn't get them, but I took some drama classes and, of course, played football. It was the night we beat UCLA. My big game, as they say. I'd just gotten back to the dorm after celebrating when Uncle Guilio reached me with the news. I thought he was calling to congratulate me."

"What happened?" Angie asked, as her grip tightened just above Jack's elbow.

"My mother had MS."

"Oh, Christ."

"Yeah. And considering how, you know, immobile she'd been for a dozen years or so, she didn't last very long. I left school and stayed with her, took about a year for her to go. Pretty fucking ugly. Before she died, she made me promise to go back to Hollywood, which I did, though I never went back to school or played football again."

"God," Angie sighed. "You've known such pain."

"Who hasn't?" Jack asked, motioning with his chin towards her, and then at the random people walking past. "Who hasn't? Sometimes I think it's the one thing we all got in common."

Angie bowed her head, staring silently at the dingy steps, before bouncing back up. "Hey!" she said and smacked Jack on the shoulder. "Enjoy your life!" she said, imitating the Chinese lady.

"I'm working on it," Jack said. He smiled and stood, pulled Angie up by both hands. They hugged among the swirling humanity, not letting go as the passing figures avoided their solitude.

*

The crowd outside the cafe where the band was to play spilled onto the street. Jack had seen them play there dozens of times, and the crowds that night were four times larger than ever before. Jack and Angie mulled for a moment around the far corner on First Avenue before walking away. The bear-in-the-chair let them through the gated fence, and they secured their luggage from the van before searching in the night for a place to call home.

The Holiday Inn on West Broadway, just above Canal, was technically SoHo but had been unofficially annexed to Chinatown – much like Little Italy already. It offered a clean room and a convenient location to hideaway for a night or two. They decided to stay in New York for a while, switching neighborhoods and boroughs every few days.

They spent their time exploring the city, delving into neighborhood after neighborhood, drinking in cafes and bars eating in restaurants, enjoying music in small clubs, finding beauty in museums and in the parks and on the streets. They wore hokey tourist t-shirts, rode double decker sight-seeing buses, visited landmarks, and attended plays on and off and way-off Broadway. They sat in movie theaters for entire rainy afternoons. They rode subways, sometimes, but mostly they walked: window shopping, shopping-shopping, and people watching around the sensory-stimulating streets. On a stormy day in Spanish Harlem, they crashed a Dominican social club, and got drunk on Brugal rum with some old timers, playing dominoes and sharing plates of roasted pork.

They made love all the time. And they did so with an intimacy and vigor and consideration for one another that would have been of no interest, and no understanding, to anyone but themselves. As a rule, they did not do the following: turn on the TV, read the newspaper, check texts or voice messages. Absolved from technology, they were ghosts in modern America, only alive for each other and the passing acquaintances of their spectral days in New York City.

There was a preternatural ease to Jack, an innate confidence with an electricity underneath which Angie first noticed on stage. People caught their breath when he entered a scene. It was far more prominent in real life, and only enhanced by his athletic fluidity, sharp charm, and angular, exotic beauty of tinted olive skin and green eyes. It stirred something unknown in those struck by his presence. He seemed, to Angie, like a romantic rebel, the kind manufactured in the movies but rarely existing in real life. He was Gatsby in a jean jacket; Sinatra in steel-toed boots.

Jack was overwhelmed by the prosaic aspects of Angelica Lightman, how real she was within her surreal existence. He admired her honesty and insight and pragmatism. He loved the way she critiqued the plays and films they saw. She was also more clever in conversation than any person he had ever known. They seemed to feed off each other that way. Jack liked that. And the fact that such attributes had blossomed in a woman of extraordinarily privileged looks and background astonished Jack more than anything else. And he was not a man easily astonished.

After a Circle Line boat tour around Manhattan, on the sparkling water that surrounded the city and provided such a distinct vantage point, Angie decided they should never leave. They'd lease a small apartment on an out of the way block in an out of the way neighborhood and walk every inch of the city for as long as it took. Then do it over again. They could make a film about it. A daring, beautiful and naive notion, tempting as it was unrealistic, imaginable yet out of reach, and dashed against the rocks of reality when obligation and California called.

*

"They're coming back," is all Major Sincoff said to Richard Evans, as if they were mid-conversation, not in the opening moment of one.

Seated across a pile of paper and crumbs from the Major, Richard chewed his tongue, afraid it would betray him. He had heeded the Major's call, certain this trip to his shit-sty of an office would end in termination. Instead, the tone suggested a collaboration of sorts, or, at least, not a foot in the ass booting him out the door and onto the pitiless street.

"Um, who's coming back?" Richard asked, wincing at the potential of sabotaging his lifeline.

The Major's face shrunk and grew blubbery, searing indignation spewing from the slits of his eyes. He grabbed a limp magazine and threw it at Richard.

FLIGHTMAN'S STILL AT LARGE read the headline. A picture of Angelica Lightman holding her Oscar was positioned next to a separate photo of Jack standing tall, football cocked in his left arm, looking down field among the assault of encroaching opponents.

"Hey," Richard said with rare enthusiasm. "I took that picture."

"Of the broad?"

"No, when I was at USC, I used to take pictures during the games and try to sell them to the school to use for promotion. That's the only one that they bought."

"Good for you," Major grunted, "but what I need is pictures of them now, together. Understand? You know, but one with that artistic touch of yours."

Richard fingered through the magazine, trying to appear interested, but his tongue got the best of him again. "How come?"

The Major pounded the table, bouncing paper and crumbs. Coffee swirled over the edge of the cup and gathered in a tawny puddle. "Have you been on fucking Mars?"

"Um, no," Richard answered, dodging a flying white spittle that shot from the corner of the Major's raging lips.

"Then you should know why this Flightman story is the only story in America today. After what happened at the radio station, Bernard Golden's has gone mental over that guy, and he was already insane over the broad, and then with them popping up in Boston, posing for pictures like that, then disappearing, it's gorgeous. People love the cat and mouse shit, not to mention the sex and violence. This Flightman thing has it all, and we need to get on board."

"Flightman?"

"Holy fucking *maschugina*," the Major moaned, running his hands over the limp ring of hair that lined the side of his grotesque head. "Flaherty plus Lightman equals Flightman, which also sums up their cowardice, running from the media as if they don't know it's us who makes them, not the other way around. They even have a logo. You know, like that basketball player jumping thing, but instead it's their figures fleeing. Pretty fucking clever, if you ask me,"

Richard blinked back a response, committed to silence this time.

"Look, stupid," the Major continued. "The only reason I hired you and the only reason I keep you around is that, once in a while, on occasion, that fucking useless talent of yours comes through, but this is your last chance. You get me some pictures of that goddamn couple, and I mean good fucking pictures, artistic pictures, not like the shit everyone else will be going for, or you'll never work around here again. In fact, I'll see to it that you never work anywhere again."

As insecure and naive as Richard was feeling at that moment, the Major's antiquated, absurd threat almost seemed plausible, though he also felt the hum of validation in his system, having been singled out for his artistry. "Um, are we sure they're coming to LA?" he asked.

"Damn sure. He's got a movie premiere on Thursday. They're coming in on a flight this afternoon, 2:30, LAX."

"No airline?"

"What do you want to do, walk up and introduce you to them? It's a private fucking plane, and there's an access area where only authorized vehicles can go. Find the spot, find a way in, and find a way to get me my fucking pictures."

"How do you know all this?" Richard asked with feigned envy.

"It's my job, shit bird," The Major scowled. "Now go do yours."

*

At Burbank's small, private airport, Walter was waiting on the tarmac in cutoff jeans, sandals, and a sleeveless rugby jersey. With aviator sunglasses in place and a boat captain's hat, he leaned against a black Mercedes sedan with his thick arms crossed. The small jet glided to a stop off the hazy runway. Heatwaves rose from the asphalt. Blasts of light reflected over every shiny surface. A small team of workers secured the wheels and waited for the cabin to open. When the door folded open, a metal stairwell was rolled into place. Angie and Jack walked into the blistering California afternoon.

Jack felt the heat tear at his scalp immediately, like he was being skinned. Angie hid under the wide brim of a straw hat. Walter waved and approached smiling, silently greeting the couple on the last step with kisses on each cheek for Angie and a warm handshake and pat on the back for Jack. He took their bags and loaded them into the trunk as Jack and Angie walked through the hot wind among roaring jet engines of the airport, disappearing into the back seat of the car behind tinted windows where it was cold as a restaurant's walk-in refrigerator.

As the car eased forward Walter adjusted the rear view mirror to see his passengers in back. "Quite a week you had, wasn't it?"

"It was…magical," Angie sighed, resting her head on Jack's shoulder.

"Well, you didn't miss much here."

"No?"

"Had a scuffle at the pub every night, which was good fun, though I think the secret's out about your spot."

"You figure?"

"Yeah," he winked into the mirror. "At least business is up."

"Did Spence stop by?" Angie asked.

"Sure did, just last night. And he was bloody adamant about hearing from either of you two." He caught Jack's eye in the rear view. "Especially you."

Jack fished through his bag and pulled out the cellphone Spence had given him which seemed like ages ago. He held down the button and watched the silver apple come to life.

"Said he left you bout near 50 messages."

Jack's phone came to life with a bong. "27 actually," he confirmed. "Jesus." He put the phone back in his pocket without turning it off.

"Not so sad, considering," Walter countered.

"Considering what?" Angie asked.

"Well, the video, of course."

Jack and Angie exchanged a portentous glance.

"Christ almighty," Walter sighed. "I thought you were hiding in New York, not Pluto."

Walter explained to Jack and Angie how a video of the events at the Bernie Golden Show had been leaked. Ramcin airs late night video from the show via one of their cable channels, and, in all the kerfuffle, the crew had managed to kill the radio mics but not the video camera. The show never aired that night, but a few days later the video was anonymously leaked, and it was not pretty, especially for Bernie Golden and Big Sid Fortunato who managed to look both cowardly and pathetic, respectively. Jack Flaherty, on the other hand, came off like an action hero, but in real fucking life. The 30 second video of his nimble move over the table, his swift cutting across the studio, his expert shattering of Bernie's protective glass followed by his deft handling of Sid had shut down the YouTube server on three occasions in two days. It had also caused volume problems at over a dozen Social Media platforms. The ink dedication attempted to keep pace.

"Oh my," Angie muttered with a component of awe threaded through the lament.

Jack slouched down in his seat and felt the world shrinking and the heat of California rise.

"Serves the bastards right," Angie said sorrowfully, snuggling her head deeper into Jack's shoulder, taking his hands in hers. After passing through a gated area, the sedan looped around the quiet roads devoid of traffic. The tops of palm trees quivered in the heat as they rolled unmolested through Burbank's glimmering streets before merging onto the highway.

"Where we going anyway?" Jack asked.

"The safest place to be in Los Angeles," Angie answered.

"And where's that?"

"Why, Santa Barbara, of course. Over ninety miles away, just past Neverland."

*

Richard had found the posse of photographers at LAX. They formed a cluster around an area in the outer reaches of the massive international airport, a fenced-off area of nothing but tarmac and trailers and dormant private jets. There was no camaraderie among the men, only clutched cameras and smartphones. Richard had driven around the airport for an hour before finding the location for private jets. He had parked his rusted Civic too far away and walked through the cement desert of the airport's ramparts. His shirt was soaked through and his hair hung limp across his forehead, sweat dripped off his long, thin nose, but he was on time: 10:00 a.m. sharp.

The other photographers made Richard nervous. They seemed swarthy, like desperate men, European criminals, or Israeli spies. They grew more agitated as the arrival time passed. Richard felt a panic attack settling into his chest. He had difficulty breathing and remembered childhood bouts with asthma. He moved away from the group and sat down on the hot ground, his back turned to the sun, leaning into a cyclone fence. He covered his face with pale, slender hands and rubbed the dust and disgust from his eyes.

The sound of a small engine arrived around 10:30. The men watched it glide towards the runway, touching ground with a chirp before taxiing to within a stone's throw from the fence. Cameras were checked and lifted and aimed by men with the fervor of feverish dogs. The doors opened and a stairwell was fastened onto the tarmac. Richard feel sick from the heat and sick from the light as he lifted his camera into place, aiming it through the chain link, intent on capitalizing on his distinct angle to capture the image of the actors as they debarked and first touched California ground. Two figures moved down the steps, a male and female, the female leading the way, her high-heel touching ground. SNAP.

Richard had taken a magnificent picture of a lovely woman of absolutely no importance whatsoever. When he looked to the pool of photographers, he noticed that most of them had begun sprinting back to where their cars had been parked in a makeshift lot. The phone in Richard's pocket vibrated. He had three text messages from the Major's assistant: THEY ARE ON THE 101 HEADING NORTH. FIND THEM!!

The photographers' cars screeched the baked concrete as they tore off towards the airport's exit. Richard thought of his rusty Civic nearly on the other side of the airport. He sat down again, leaning against the fence, his hands, once again, covering his face, his fingers rubbing his eyes, where the tears mingled with dust.

*

The Mercedes sedan crept along in midday traffic. Walter's foot tapped impatiently on the accelerator. He gripped the steering wheel with the resolve of a strangler. He checked the rear view frequently, as if he were in danger of a speeding ticket.

Jack and Angie held hands in the back seat and looked out separate windows as the landscape of tract housing and open sky slowly moved past. There was no shoulder, only a slope of grass towards the thick soundproof fences that bordered the identical backyards. The only sound was the whoosh of the air conditioning and a car horn orchestra from behind them. Angie imagined impatient drivers to their rear. Jack reminded himself of his hatred for LA's vehicular reality.

A burst of volume traffic caused the sedan to stop altogether. Angie sighed and traced circles around one of Jack's knuckles when Walter abruptly switched lanes. The car he cut off blew its horn. Walter watched the rear view more than the road ahead. He made another aggressive move, and it now seemed the cars in their company were gathering against them with their collective honking.

"Relax, love," Angie said is a soothing voice. "You'll be free to commence your rally soon enough."

"It's not that," he said, eyes once again on the mirror. "I think we're being followed."

Jack and Angie both sat up, leaning towards the front of the car.

"Why would you think that?" Angie asked, a trill of panic in her voice.

"There," Walter said, motioning with his head towards the rear view. "That red Mustang behind and to the left, fought its way up here from as far back as I could see and now it seems happy to stay put."

Jack and Angie turned to the back window, looking through the darkened glass at the lone, male driver of the Mustang. The visor in front of him was down, though the sun blasted from behind.

"And there," Walter continued. "Back about two lengths. That white Malibu has been right aggressive, as well."

Horns erupted as a third car, a sporty tan Fiat, slipped in off the non-existent shoulder into the spot directly behind the sedan.

"Oh, Christ," Angie sighed, her hand clutching Jack's palm.

"Any advice, M'lady?" Walter asked.

"Lose them," Angie ordered, as she slunk down into the cushioned seats. "I guess."

And so began possibly the slowest car chase in history. On the gridlocked 101, the black sedan nudged its way through traffic while the red mustang, white Malibu and tan Fiat stayed no further than a vehicle or two behind. There was just no losing them. At one point, they had the sedan surrounded on three sides. California law only allowed for tint to be applied to back windows, so the pursuers tried valiantly to get slightly ahead of the sedan in order to peer into the backseat.

The tension wrenched at Angie, who frequently pounded on the seat beside her while staring furiously into the back of the seat before her eyes. Jack leaned over the passenger seat, and futilely scanned the horizon for means of escape. The passenger in the pursuit cars even held the camera up at times, teasing the trapped prey. When the Malibu slammed the back fender, Jack lurched from his seat, reaching for the door.

"Don't!" Angie demanded. "That's what they want."

"The fuck do we do?" he asked, his voice rising and accent appearing. "They'll follow us all the way to Santa Barbara."

"Allow me to stop the car and get wicked on their asses, M'lady?" Walter asked, his ears shading red, his massive hands clenching at the wheel.

Angie could see the intensity in Jack's eyes, the anger underneath his cool veneer, as if it had been stored in the bottom of a well but now rising. She squeezed his hand and acknowledged his pain. As outraged as she also was, she did not want to see Jack in any more trouble or allow the kind of carnage Walter would certainly produce once let loose on the paparazzi. It was time for her to take charge.

"Last night," Angie asked of Walter, "did you inform Spencer of our arrival time?"

"Certainly did, M'lady," he said. "10:00 a.m. sharp at LAX. Burbank never came up. I'm certain."

Jack began to study Walter's eyes in the rear view, when Angie grabbed his arm.

"Give me your phone."

"What?"

"Your phone. It's on, I presume."

Jack fished in his pocket for the new phone and handed it to Angie. She quickly held down the power button, slid the prompt to turn it off.

"This is how they found us. GPS. Spence must have you tracked. When we didn't arrive at LAX, he tracked you using this and phoned his sources."

She smirked as Jack furrowed his brow and felt his hairline sprinkle with shame.

"Bloody 'ell," Walter seethed. "His next meal at the pub is going to have a fair amount of short and curlies in it."

"We'll deal with dear Spencer soon enough," Angie said. "The key for now is find our way out of this spot without getting killed in the process."

The Malibu nudged them again from behind. This time with more force.

"The key is to stay calm," Angie murmured. "To stay calm and think."

Jack found his breath and joined in the brainstorming. They lurched forward for a matter of minutes before the silence was promptly broken.

"I've got it!" Angie cried.

The two passengers awaited her response.

"Fried eggs," she said and began to climb into the front seat. "Fried fucking eggs."

*

The studio of Bernie Golden's show was electric. The host himself was pacing behind the partition of his newly repaired throne, stroking his cross bow. The lackeys, with the exception of Leonard, were upright in their chairs, practically swallowing their microphones. Jerry D was on his cell phone, listening intently while holding up a hand to keep his audience at bay.

"We got 'em," Bernie said with a curled lip. "We fucking got 'em."

Smoov hit the cash register sound effect.

"They thought that they could hide," Bernie continued. His voice was exaggerated, engaging in a false and cryptic narrative, but his message was freighted with a sad seriousness that belied the dramatics. "But we got 'em. They are our prisoners. They belong to us because without us they would not exist."

"So, how's this gonna play out, boss?" Sid, the 300-pound dilettante, asked.

Bernie didn't respond at first or even acknowledge the question. He continued his prowl with his head pointed towards the floor. Then he spoke in a prophetic tone: "The highway will open up soon and a chase will ensue. It'll be like O.J. all over again, running for his life on the fucking California freeway. Beautiful. Jerry, you working on that helicopter?"

The producer, still on the phone, nodded vigorously.

Bernie Golden rubbed his hands together.

"It'll be just like the O.J. hustle. That gorgeous fiasco, except there will be the press in hot pursuit, just like Lady Di, and we'll have the two biggest celebrity crackups in history mixed into one. It'll be a thing of beauty," he muttered in a guttural rasp. "A fucking thing of beauty."

The cash register chimed; the echoing sound of the bell hung in the air for a few long, stilted seconds.

"Ah, boss mang," Smoov queried. "You don't really want anyone to get hurt, do you, mang?"

Bernie Golden turned to his crew. Leonard Temple felt relieved the program was not captured on film because the face of the host, plastered with malevolence, belied his simple statement of "Of course not, retard. I just want to give the people what they want – pictures of animals in the zoo."

*

Bernie Golden grew up in a dilapidated track house in the foothills of a Nevada exurb. His father, with greasy hair and greasy hands, owned a filling station; his mother, a comely and ageless cocktail waitress, ran off with a drunkard of a traveling salesman from Kansas City when Bernie was 15 years old. By that time, he'd quit school and was on the motocross circuit full time. He lived off decent racing winnings and small confidence scams around the southwest. He settled in Vegas after breaking his leg in a horrific motocross accident, where his femur had pierced his thigh, that left him with a limp that young Bernie adapted into a gate.

In Vegas, he quickly became a recognized entity, a local character, lanky and bombastic, cowboy boots and chewed matchsticks, a pompadour of auburn hair. He could be found leaning into any given bar on any given night, looking for backroom card games, unsuspecting yokels to scam or pimping runaways from middle America to bachelor parties on a budget. He had a room at the Excelsior Motel, first floor beside the filmy pool, at the far end of the Vegas Strip, and a line of credit at a few of the smaller casinos. There were ties to local hustlers and a white supremacist group, and he was even questioned about the shooting of Tupac Shakur on the Las Vegas Strip. But Bernie Golden was more of a local character than a big time player. To the serious criminal element he was simply too extroverted, too caustic, to be brought inside. So Bernie, in the dawn of the 21st century, worked the fringes of the Vegas underbelly until serendipity arrived in the form of the Hollywood's highest paid sitcom actor who came to town on an epic bender.

Bernie was sipping tequila, tweaking on crystal meth, at the bar of the Bellagio Hotel around 3:00 in the morning when a plump prostitute from Texarkana sauntered up in cutoff jeans and a frayed halter top looking like she just swallowed a canary.

She smiled and dropped a leather wallet on the bar.

"You familiar with this man?" she asked.

Bernie opened the wallet and checked the cash sleeve, which was empty. The prostitute smirked at Bernie and rolled her eyes at his foolishness. Bernie studied the driver's license and recognized the person in the picture immediately.

"He's a damn mess," she said. "Been doing lines of coke non-stop for the better part of three days, and from what I understand, he's been through about a dozen girls and god knows how much cocaine. Not to mention a lot of Viagra. He's afraid to leave the room, so he sends the girl he's done with out to get the next one. That pretty black girl, the one that dances over at Cheetah, she saw me down by the diner and told me to go on up. I hardly recognized him at first, he so torn up, but that's him alright. I only been there about ten minutes 'fore he done fall asleep with his tired ole' dicky in my mouth. So I grabbed his wallet and git."

"You don't fuckin' say," Bernie muttered indifferently, though his mind raced.

The prostitute said, "Why don't you do *sumpthing* with them credit cards before he wakes up and cancels 'em? You and me go even-Steven on the proceeds. Fair enough?"

Bernie rummaged through the wallet.

"I got a better idea," he said, pulling out the hotel room's card for entry. "You remember the room number?"

Bernie Golden and the plump prostitute from Texarkana stopped by the gift shop and then went up to the top-floor accommodation of the binge-bleary sitcom actor. He was blacked out on the couch of his darkened two-room suite, pants around his ankles and the twinkling Technicolor lights of Las Vegas beyond his askance head. The room smelled of sex and body odor and baby oil. The TV flickered from an overnight loop of SportsCenter, casting the actor in a ghostly blue glow.

Bernie turned on all the overhead lights. The glass table in front of the slumbering actor was covered in the detritus of a modern Bacchanalian bender: a bag of cocaine, a bag of Viagra, a box of condoms, baby oil, bananas, Red Bull, Grey Goose, a bucket of melted ice, a credit card and a rolled up $50 bill in a bed of Peruvian powder.

Bernie took the credit card and slivered out a long line, which he snorted through one of the rolled up bill. He sniffed in the remnants then gave the $50 to the plump prostitute, which she licked then pocketed.

"What's with the bananas?" Bernie asked.

"I hear he likes to put them in the girls while he waiting for the Viagra to kick in. Front and back."

"Hmmm," Bernie hummed, removing the disposable camera from the gift shop bag. "Let's do this."

The next morning the beleaguered actor woke up alone on the coach of his two-room suite in the Bellagio Hotel. He squinted against the natural light that mercilessly poured through the floor to ceiling windows that surrounded the suite on three sides. All the overhead lights were on, as well. He was naked, except for a tourist t-shirt, which he didn't remember buying or putting on. It smelled new. The glass table that had held his assorted components of contraband was empty, except for a white photo envelope with a CVS logo. His wrists were raw, and his rectum ached as he stumbled over to the windows to draw the shades. In the cool of the newly-shaded room, Hollywood's top paid sitcom star sat back down onto the couch of his two room suite and, despite his raw wrists and aching rectum, considered himself lucky. At least he was alive and alone and aware of his surroundings. Safe. He'd gotten whatever he needed to get out of his system. He was checking out that morning, getting his Thunderbird out of the garage below the hotel, and taking that drive across the desert to his Malibu mansion, where he'd sit in the sauna and purge for as long as it took to feel remotely whole again. He'd go on a cabbage diet for a week. Call his trainer. Call his manager and apologize for those awful things he'd said before leaving for Las Vegas. Maybe meet him for lunch again in Beverly Hills, listen to what he had to say this time about rehab. They say you have to hit rock bottom before you can begin to rise. He'd officially hit rock bottom. But somehow survived. This was it. Everything was going to be alright. He'd been to hell, and now it was time for the back again part. Hollywood's highest paid sitcom star ran a hand through his mangled head of thick brown hair and breathed through his perfect nose. He began to count his blessings when the toilet flushed.

Well, maybe one more romp, he thought, assuming he still had hired company on hand. He felt the blood stir in his loins, and he hoped, in the bathroom, it was the black chic with the long legs he remembered from late last night. Or was it the night before? His breath quickened and his cock stiffened as the water ran in the bathroom sink and then stopped. He inhaled with anticipation as the bathroom door keened, but gusted out disappointment and fear when out came a strange man with an auburn pompadour, chewing on a matchstick. The actor's pores opened and toxins began to ooze as shock coursed through his ravaged nervous system.

"Good morning there, partner," Bernie Golden said, striding in an awkward gate across the suite towards the living area. "Thought you might never wake up."

"The, the fuck are you?" the actor asked with a hoarse, quivering voice, his throat starting to burn from sinus damage as his cock shriveled.

"Like I said," Bernie chirped, approaching with his hand out and a shit-eating grin spread across his sallow, pink face. "Your new partner. Partner."

The wind whipped across Bernie's face as he sat in the front seat of the sitcom actor's convertible Thunderbird as they raced across the desert towards LA. He was surprised by the actor's lack of resistance to his plan, as if he were familiar with the process of being blackmailed. Though, Bernie had to admit, the pictures he'd taken were pretty damn compelling. He'd had them developed after dropping off the plump prostitute from Texarkana as the sun came up after their fashion shoot with the blacked out sitcom star and all of his assorted props. She had wanted to invite a bunch of her friends up, make a party out of it, but Bernie knew the less people involved the better. The key was keeping this just between them. He wouldn't even let the girl herself into the picture; instead, she served as his assistant, helping pose the actor in various positions. She'd done the honors with the banana, too.

After confiscating all the paraphernalia, Bernie insisted on driving the plump prostitute home to the listing bungalow she shared with a couple other girls on the ramparts of town. She kept insisting on taking a cab, using the pocket full of the actor's cash she helped herself to, but

Bernie insisted in his most convincing and gentlemanly tone. The same one he used on yokels or lame bachelor parties in the midst of his scams. When they got to her house, he noted the address and let her know sincerely that he'd be in touch very soon. He made her promise not to say a single word or all their certain riches would be lost. He promised her, that if she kept her mouth closed, she'd soon have enough money to do whatever she wanted. She wanted to buy a place of her own in Galveston, right on the Gulf of Mexico. Bernie assured her that was a wonderful idea before driving back towards town.

He went to his bank and withdrew his life savings of some $8,000 and called, from a payphone on the Strip, a degenerate button man he drank with on occasion. Bernie returned to his room at the Excelsior Motel and packed up a trash bag with all the belongings he could fit before checking out, telling the manager to put his deposit towards the removal of all the crap he'd left behind. At a Staples near the strip, he bought a metal briefcase into which he packed most of his cash. He left the briefcase with a Laundromat operator and trusted fence and then went to get his pictures developed at a CVS. He kindly told the pimple-faced kid running the photo section that the pictures were of the most personal nature and that if he even so much as caught a glimpse of them he'd have his balls on a stick as soon as his shift ended.

Convinced of the photo developer's innocence, Bernie drove back to the Bellagio with one set of pictures in a CVS envelope, the other sitting safely in a locker at bus station in the heart of Vegas. He used the actor's room key to access the top floor via the hotel elevator and enter the suite. He tossed the envelope on the glass table and made himself comfortable until the slumbering actor awoke, which he did while Bernie was using the facilities.

They were now partners, riding together towards LA, crossing the desert together with the wind whipping Bernie's face as he wondered if the plumb prostitute from Texarkana was dead yet and what Los Angeles had in store for him.

Bernie set up shop in the actor's pool house. An adobe bungalow of two rooms with a lofted sleeping space, nestled between the large kidney-shaped pool and clay tennis courts, across a yawning blue lawn from the mansion itself of white plaster with nine bedrooms and ten baths beneath the terracotta tiled roof. The house also held a bowling alley, a movie theater, and a grand room with a long mahogany bar and billiards tables, a roulette wheel, and a DJ station. The towering trees and dense vegetation that surrounded the estate were threaded with a 20-foot electric fence and a state of the art security system. No neighbors. The only way in was through a massive wrought iron gate at the bottom of a long drive. On the night of festivities, armed security worked the gate and roamed the grounds. A team of servers were brought in to tend to the revelers who conducted themselves like it was spring break in ancient Athens.

Bernie Golden, with his Vegas-informed taste for depravity, found the events distasteful. The party-goers were a ménage of B-actors, reality stars, doppelgangers, drug dealers, groupies, flunkies, crappy musicians, Playboy castoffs, and porn stars. Bernie liked the porn crowd the best. They arrived early and were the last to leave, often bringing up the sun floating on rafts, high and giddy, in the expansive pool that fronted Bernie's abode. And while he found some camaraderie with the porn industry, the entertainment industry types disgusted him. Despite his considerable gift of gab, Bernie was unable to establish any rapport with a type of people who were entirely self-important and inherently uninteresting, comprised of elitists and hacks and idiots. All of them talent-less phonies, much like his benefactor, who made the type of money 10 guys like him together wouldn't see in 10 lifetimes. They were, to a person, entirely undeserving of the heaping attention, riches, and sense of self-importance in which they wallowed. It offended him. Deeply. Bernie tagged along for a while to other people's parties or exclusive clubs or power lunches, where he was treated as a pariah or ignored entirely, his bad leg and his bad looks now a noticeable handicap. If people paid him any attention at all, it was to sneer or wonder, aloud, who he was and why he was there.

Bernie seethed. The rejection corroded him. He thought about selling the pictures of the actor to one of the tabloid magazines, living as long as he could in Mexico off the proceeds. Then he thought again. He made a deal with the actor: He would stop attending his parties and accompanying him around town, even move out of the guest house, eliminating all apparent ties whatsoever, in exchange for gossip on fellow actors, scoop on their addresses, whereabouts, misadventures. He wanted war. He started a website called STALKER as his weapon.

In the fledgling 21st century, in the immediate aftermath of still-traumatized post-9/11 world, of potential terrorist plots and mushroom clouds and anthrax in the mail, in an age of dawning technology and corporate media conglomeration, Bernie Golden's jihad against Hollywood was perfectly timed. It was an absurdists' paradise. The lowest common denominator was at a premium. He became the primary source of information for the booming celebrity-culture tabloids and newscasts. He regularly pranked celebrities, all caught on film. He created a collection of sex tapes staring fledgling actors and his porn star friends, disguised as groupies interested in innocent sex, destroying many careers on the rise. He crashed parties with midgets and stuntmen and degenerates he'd found on the streets of the Sunset Strip. He thrived on humiliation, and was creating a fortune for himself and a unique place of power in celebrity America.

Bernie's status remained until Barack Obama announced his candidacy for President of the United States, and the reality of this potential was made real to many when Hollywood invited the African-American senator from the state of Illinois for a record-shattering fundraiser in the hills of Hollywood, California. The event was arranged and hosted by the actress Angelica Lightman. The whole thing – this half-black novice and this half-American bitch getting so much attention - drove Bernie Golden crazy.

He sold STALKER to a tabloid subsidiary and went to work independently as a clandestine political operative. His efforts affected congressional races in the next four elections cycles. In a second decade of the new century, his maneuverings played a large role in the derailment of two Democratic Senate candidates: one going down in a white hot scandal; the other, wisely, backing out in the 11th hour for undisclosed personal reasons, handing the chamber's majority to the Republican party. As a reward, Bernie Golden was given his own radio program via a Chinese multinational corporation, which was one of the Republican parties most generous donors, where he, aided by FCC deregulations, continued his ribald jihad against celebrity activists in general and Angelica Lightman in particular, pacing around his studio, many years later, waiting for news of the actress' capture on the 101 Freeway heading north towards Santa Barbara.

*

Once in the front passenger seat, Angie had unfastened her bra and removed it all together. It fell to the floor board by her feet. Walter and Jack exchanged glances, but neither said a word. The honking had increased on the highway as the sedan and its three pursuers jockeyed slowly yet with great aggression down the 101. They were all behind the sedan and to the left. There was an exit about 200 yards up on the right.

As the sedan slowly approached vehicles on the passenger side, Angie waited for a solitary male driver. She had turned the visor to the window, to hide the identity of her face, and she kept her profile concealed as best she could with both hands firmly grasping the hem of her shirt.

"Walter," she said with great care. "When we come upon this next vehicle, be prepared to cut in front of him instantly, the second he stops."

"And how do we know he's going to stop?"

"I'm not certain of it, but I suspect he will." There was a bouncing silliness to her face, though Angie's eyes remained focused.

The sedan inched forward and was soon upon an emerald BMW piloted by a lone man in his 30s wearing a golf shirt and aviator sunglasses. Angie waited until they were perfectly parallel, then sprang into action, pulling up her shirt and pressing her breasts into the passenger side window. Her large breast flattened out into perfect circles with her round nipples forming an inner circle.

Jack watched from the anonymity of the back seat as the driver noticed Angie's fried egg impression upon the passenger window.

"Now!" Jack ordered a second before the driver did a double take and instinctively touched on his breaks. The sedan slid safely in front of the BWM just before it lurched back into motion. Angie screamed like a school girl from the front seat; Jack slapped his leg and howled.

"I'll be," Walter muttered, his eyes watching the traffic stall behind him.

They'd distanced themselves a few lengths from their pursuers, who aggressively tried to make up ground, but the cars around them seemed to stand ground, to become equally as aggressive. A game of sorts had ensued.

The next fellow traveler to be served up a heaping portion of fried eggs was a man in a Lexus wearing a business suit talking into his cell phone. It took him a minute to notice the dish being served up to his peripheral vision, but when he noticed, the shock sent his foot to the brake pedal with such force that the car behind rear-ended him as the sedan made another move forward and to the right.

The exit was now 50 yards away as the sedan slipped up against a farmer in a dusty pickup truck. The man behind the wheel, a septuagenarian in a flannel shirt and baseball hat with a curved brim, nodded at the entrée on display in the adjacent window, slowed his vehicle to a crawl and motioned with his hand, in a gentlemanly fashion, for the sedan to proceed ahead of him. Angie blew him a kiss as Walter jerked in front of him and onto the small shoulder which fed the exit ramp.

Walter, as if freed from a cage, pinned the gas pedal and flew down the exit ramp. He took the curve at nearly three times the recommended speed, taking all the German engineering the Mercedes afforded to keep from flipping. The car shimmied sideways, jolting the passengers in a stuttering fashion. With the car on steady ground and slightly slower, it only had to go from 60 to 0 in 3.5 seconds to avoid the rushing traffic on the avenue fed by the exit. Walter slammed on the breaks and centrifugal force lunged through the car from the rear. Jack reached over from the back seat, to keep Angie, unfastened from her seat belt, from meeting the dashboard. All three passengers had been jarred by the abrupt stop.

"Good lord, Walter!" Angie screamed. "Calm the right fuck down!"

"Sorry," he mumbled, staring at the steering wheel. "Sorry."

""'No time for apologies," Jack said, looking out the back window. "Here comes the Fiat."

Walter looked up, his eyes alive once again. He hit the gas and shot across the busy boulevard. A swarm of oncoming traffic approached from the left. Angie screamed and covered her face, curled up on her seat. Jack ducked behind her seat, bracing for impact. Walter pounded the accelerator and swept just past the rush of traffic, skidding sideways onto the nearest lane of the road heading north, barely avoiding the grill of an 18-wheeler that had been merging left to exit. The Fiat was unable to successfully navigate the oncoming traffic and was stalled, blocked in by cars that had locked on their brakes to avoid Walter's mad dash. The Mercedes soared off towards the north on a pedestrian boulevard.

"Sorry about that, M'lady," Walter said, bolstered a bit by the escape but shaken by his imprudence.

Angie scurried into the backseat and strapped her safety belt. "Jesus Christ, Walter! My God, what has gotten into you? You're a loon, but never this bloody crazy!"

The chastised driver shrugged and drove ahead at a steady clip.

"Well, don't attempt that again," Angie scolded, cooling a bit around the edges. "I'd rather get my photo snapped than die a bloody death."

"Understood, M'lady."

Angie sighed and leaned back into the plush seats.

"I bet we could all go for a cocktail, eh?" she suggested.

Walter gave a big nod into the rear view.

"Yeah," Jack said, but we should probably pay a visit to Spence first."

"Right," Angie agreed. "Turn it around will you, Walter, take us back to town. We need a word with dear Spencer."

"I can get us to Santa Barbara on the backgrounds from here. No fuss," Walter said, a slight quiver in his voice. "Let's put this mess behind us and belly up for a bit."

"Not yet," Angie said, her eyes fixed out the window on the cactus and the sage that grew in the median.

Walter's shoulders sagged as he put the sedan in gear, drove under the overpass and turned onto the ramp in the direction of the LA bound freeway as a low-flying helicopter zoomed overhead, going in the other direction.

*

"How ya' doing, Mona?" Jack asked, walking into the Berman Agency office with Angie and Walter in tow.

Mona stood up behind her desk as if she had just been caught stealing. "Where have you been?" she asked. "Spence has lost his mind!"

"Is he in?" Jack asked casually, motioning towards his closed door.

"Yes, but he's on the phone…"

They walked past her without word, pushing through the door and into the office glittering with testimony to Spence's success, a testimony to Spence himself. He tore off his earphone, bolting from his cushy seat. "Where in the hell have you been?" he asked, looking to Jack with indignation. "How do you expect me to do my job if you disappear for weeks at a time? I've got people from the studio calling me at all hours…"

His diatribe was interrupted by a decorative paperweight Angie seized from a shelf and launched towards his face, thudding off the bridge of his nose. After impact, Spence cupped his face and fell back into his chair as the oblong object rebounded onto his desk top and circled in decreasing sphere shapes before settling into silence.

Jack and Angie made a two person wall at the front of the desk, as Spence stared up at them with incredulity. He took his hands away to grasp the handkerchief from his breast pocket, covering the blood that was seeping over the circle of gray beard around his mouth. "What…are…you…doing?" he asked through the dancing hankey, his eyes widened simultaneously with fear, outrage, confusion, and hurt.

"You fucking bastard!" Angie screamed, practically hurling herself over the desk. "You bloody fucking bastard!"

Spence reared back, his chair rolling in reverse until the plate glass kept him from spilling into the Burbank skyline. He held up a hand in a plea for calm, but Angie wasn't having it.

"We were almost killed today, you son of a bitch!"

She lunged for Spence, but Jack held her back with a grip around her elbow and another around her waist. She reached out as if to scratch out his eyes.

Deeply wounded and terribly frightened, Spence sought out Angie with his eyes, a look freighted with familiarity and a plea for compassion, but by then she had broken down: The anger finally subsiding, replaced by deep, paralyzing sickness about what had happened that afternoon and what had happened so often in her past; about what had happened to her life. She buried herself into Jack's chest and heaved, her composure finally breaking like a bottle. Spence's confounded eyes spoke of shock, an inability to accept what was before him.

Angie's sobs filled the office, and Jack held her like a child. Walter stood down in the back of the office, exchanging furtive glances with Mona who lingered in the threshold, her eyes muted by contrition. When she opened her mouth, Jack held up his hand, returning it tenderly to the small of Angie's back. After a climatic heave, sigh, and wail Angie stepped back from Jack, wiped her eyes with the palms of her hands, took a deep breath and looked around the room until settling her eyes on Spence.

"You, Spencer fucking Berman, are officially fired. Have at him, Walter," she said without emotion. "Kill him for all I care."

Spence gasped and banged his chair back against the window in fear of what was coming, but nothing happened. In the silence that followed, the loyal bodyguard and lifelong ally of Angelica Lightman simply blinked and breathed, looked bashfully at his shoes, for it was all he could manage. Angie knew now what Jack had suspected since the car ride and confirmed upon arrival at Spence's office. Angie bolted from the room.

Walter watched her go then, sensing danger, turned quickly back towards Jack. He was too late. A straight right punch, delivered with all the energy of Jack's torso and legs, caught the rough and tumble Brit square on the chin, sending him back a few steps and eventually to the ground. The car keys sprawled towards the door. Mona picked them up and handed them, with quivering hands, to Jack on his way past in pursuit of Angie.

*

Richard Evans danced in place, vying for space among the paparazzi that cloistered the red carpet outside Mann's Chinese Theater. The early evening air, as it often did these days, smelled metallic. He had a crappy pop song in his head, a tune that he hated, though, this evening, its bubble gum verses tinged him with joy. Most of the cast and crew of *The Killing Kind* had already walked graciously past, appreciative of the Blockbuster attention given to an art house film; but the star of top billing, nor the actor of most interest, had yet to arrive at the premiere. Jostling with his elbows, Richard was more aggressive than usual, it being unusual for him to be aggressive at all, knowing this was his latest last chance. He griped his camera with sweaty digits, and waited along the velvet rope for his moment to arrive.

There had been no word of Angelica Lightman and Jack Flaherty after their escape from the media three days earlier. No tips had come across the Major's desk, and he was uncharacteristically silent on the failure of Richard to return with any shots from the airport. He assumed that he had been given a pass since all the photographers, even those who had taken part in the ridiculous chase, had failed to procure even a single photo worthy of publication. There had been absurd pedestrian accounts of Angelica Lightman flashing her breasts at passing motorists, but the media seemed to ignore this story in large part, possibly since it was too fantastic to even consider, too glorious of a missed opportunity to highlight.

So Richard kept his job for another week and was assigned yet another attempt at redemption. He had arrived at 4:30 and had been standing in place, buttressed by a velvet rope, for two hours. He'd purposely positioned himself with the dying light to his back, using the slanted sunshine to bask upon his subjects as they exited from private cars and walked the red carpet among screams of fans and media. Richard had taken, he was certain, some lovely shots of the supporting cast as they glided past, waiving and stopping, on occasion, to talk to the glossy reporters from the entertainment shows.

Richard, like everyone else gathered outside the theater that night, felt the rise of anticipation as the evening wore on. His space was being threatened by late arriving paparazzi who had jostled their way into his domain via pointed elbows and claims of press credentials and inherent priority. But Richard held his ground and kept his spot in a prime placement a few yards up the rope from the debarking point for the stars. He had felt emboldened about this assignment for some reason, though he detested every aspect of celebrity photography. Something felt different, fateful almost, about the whole "Flightman" escapade from the beginning and especially this evening. Perhaps it was merely the light that bolstered Richard's mood.

The sun had sunk into the hills and a sparkling twilight sifted down on Hollywood. It was one of the two magic moments of day that Richard favored for his photography since the light lent itself to an atmosphere of majesty. For a few moments at dusk and a few moments at dawn, there was a stillness in the environment, as if time were suspended for just a few moments each morning and evening when the guards of time changed posts. It was when he, a perpetual outsider, felt welcome in the world.

And it was in this small window of time that a stretch Town Car pulled up to the awning at Mann's Chinese Theater, and the actor Jack Flaherty stepped out of the backseat and into the last light of a California day. He was alone and dressed in a black suit with a white dress shirt and a skinny black tie. His familiar shaved head had given way to a shadow of growth which framed his face in a more masculine way – his green eyes seemed brighter and his other angular features more pronounced. The crowd, as if drawn by this subtle yet dramatic change in appearance, surged as he walked the carpet, constricting upon the corridor for the actors to pass, but extra bodyguards arrived to hold back the tide. Richard felt a jolt of adrenaline as he raised his camera, ignoring the pressure from behind him and, more importantly, the synapse that was pulsing through his brain, giving bloom to a thought that had been dormant since the evening he first encountered this curiosity of an actor, the night outside Blue Roses when he had frozen in the light of this stranger's stare. The night that the growling Brit had broken his camera.

Richard lowered his camera. And his concept that was conceived the night at Blue Roses, which had laid restless yet dormant these passing weeks, was activated when Jack Flaherty, the man he had come to photograph, the man everyone had come to photograph, in his shiny black suit and his nascent head of hair, stopped his one-man parade down the red carpet to pause in front of Richard and stare. The two men exchanged a look of recognition, holding each other's eyes as contemporaries, as telepathic co-conspirators in a concept that exploded inside the firing imagination of Richard Evans like 4th of July fireworks. Jack nodded at the man with the drawn-down camera and the blossoming eyes, and went on his way as flashes popped and fans screamed and Richard Evans' imagination birthed the idea which launched this story.

Part II

Richard Evans, in his rusty Civic, wended down the desolate canyon passages towards Pacific Palisades. He drove slowly, his focus intense on the task of driving even though the bulk of his mental prowess was on the idea that had overwhelmed him only moments before. The idea had surely and finally cost him his job as a photo journalist, for the Major would never tolerate this last act of incompetence. The lingering notion that Richard had lost his job and pissed of the Major in the process only added to the feverish manner which his mind raced and breath came in steady streams, in and out of his nose, his eyes fixed on the undulating and serpentine lane lit by his headlights.

Richard had left the premiere without a single picture. He walked purposefully to his car, started the engine, and drove, like a perfect citizen, out of Hollywood on broken boulevards past desperate drifters and gawkers and hustlers, past the bus station he had debarked from ten years earlier, a refugee from the suburban squalor of Fresno, a recent high school graduate in search of escape and meaning, more intrigued, despite his homosexuality, by the grit and glamour of Los Angeles than the potential of acceptance and community in San Francisco.

He wanted to take pictures, for therein lie his meaning. A lonely and only child of kind yet reticent parents, he had found a place for himself in art. He sketched constantly, in his room, at the kitchen table, on the bus to school. He filled notebooks with his detailed portrayals of landscapes and architecture and, eventually, people. Inspired by the paintings of Frida Kahlo, he committed himself to self-portrait. And it was through this that he discovered his own character, his loneliness and love and desire to communicate, which eventually brought him to his muse. Richard abandoned himself as a subject and began drawing others: his parents, neighbors, classmates, teachers, pastors, strangers. He could capture their essence through his pencil, through the small details which exposed identity. When a high school art teacher introduced Richard to photography (and his homosexual desires that no drawing could reveal), he'd found his new medium.

Richard identified with the life and work of Robert Mapplethorpe, seeking to create art through photographic portraits. And while Mapplethorpe's homosexuality was somewhat validating to him, Richard greatly admired the stylish yet simple early work of the famous photographer to the more sexually provocative photos which later inspired controversy. He preferred Patti Smith on the cover of *Horses* to the bullwhip-up-the-ass stuff of *The Perfect Moment.* He especially loved the photo of Mapplethorpe and Smith together from the book jacket of Smith's memoir, former lovers and lifelong friends. He had sometimes spent whole afternoons in his room staring at it, absorbing its essence. Seeking dynamic subjects, complex and diverse yet somehow prosaic, is what brought the 19-year-old Richard from Fresno to Los Angeles. His desire, with every shot, was to capture the moment in all its depth and insight. He was after the zeitgeist. A photograph that captured the moment in time.

It had been ten years since he stepped off that bus, nervous and naive, knowing he was going to suffer, knowing he would learn to survive, anxious for the exposure and experience that would inform his art and develop his character. It had been hard. Far harder than he ever imagined. The crappy jobs and crappy apartments, wasted film and wasted time, the constant struggle of being alone. But Richard persisted. He endured heartbreak and humiliation, again and again, until an angel was delivered to him in a bath house near Venice Beach. An older gentleman, an alcoholic actor from Malibu via Brooklyn, became Richard's secret lover and benefactor. He paid for Richard's modest (yet clean and safe) apartment on Wilshire Boulevard on the Santa Monica/Brentwood border (only a few blocks from the tony neighborhood where Nicole Simpson and Ron Perlman had been murdered).

This gentleman also arranged for Richard's acceptance (and tuition) at USC's undergraduate program where he earned a BFA in Photography and validated his talent with the array of insightful portraits he took of myriad Los Angelinos: gangbangers and socialites and porn stars; skin heads, athletes, law enforcement officers and movie executives; waiters and musicians and screenwriters; immigrants and surfers and those who slept slumped against trees, buttressed by their corroded belongings. He captured as much of Los Angeles as he could, while keeping his camera away from stars of any big screen. To Richard, it was a matter of principal and a matter of art, for the portraits of celebrities told no story. He displayed his photos in an online gallery that few visited.

Shortly after graduation from USC, Richard found himself unceremoniously cut off from the drunk actors' largess, for he had spent his fortune and needed rehab. It was then that Richard – out of sheer desperation to remain in his safe and clean apartment away from the soiled Los Angeles of his earlier days – abandoned his principals: He went to work taking pictures for one of the many celebrity magazines based in LA. But not just any celebrity magazine. Richard, inspired by a spiraling sense of self-loathing, took his portfolio into the offices of one of the city's most disreputable rags, *Sellebrity Skin*. The name wasn't as noxious as some of the other rage, like *LA Ass* or *Tuna Town*, but the play on words had a sinister undertone, a not so subtle indication of the magazine's ethos.

Major Sincoff seemed cartoonish, a perfect boss of such a sleazy outfit. He hired Richard on the spot without ever shaking his hand. The salary was modest, but enough to keep Richard afloat until his breakthrough came. In the meantime, informed by the Major's tips, he stalked celebrities, especially women, charged with capturing photographs of tramp stamps and cleavage and baby bumps, cellulite and stomach rolls, bad hair days and wardrobe malfunctions. He did well enough to keep his job, to pay the bills and keep taking his own pictures, holding out until his time arrived.

And after ten years of Los Angeles living, it arrived at last. It arrived after putting his camera dawn and acknowledging an idea, one that was unknowingly conceived a few weeks prior, outside of a restaurant on a celebrity stalk, during another impotent attempt at the kind of photography Richard loathed. And now he drove in his rusted Civic through the hills and canyons of Pacific Palisades towards that very spot where the inkling of an idea was first aroused. He turned sharply into the gravel drive of Blue Roses, the modest ranch tucked away in a barren of pines. The parking lot was empty, save for a topless and antique Range Rover aside a Laurel tree by the front entrance. The restaurant was dark, but a dull glow emanated through the pained-window of the front door, which was unlocked. Richard entered a dark foyer and through a thick curtain into the bar area, where the raving Brit who had smashed his camera a few weeks before sat at the bar watching a rugby match on the television while sipping a pint of beer through a straw. He turned his hostile eyes on Richard and growled through clenched jaws, "The fucking 'ell you want?"

*

Two days later, Richard walked, uninvited, into the office of Major Sincoff at *Sellebrity Skin*. People had parted when Richard passed through the dim office. They looked at him with pity, like he was on his way to his own execution: Dead Man Walking. Richard *was* actually concerned with his own physical safety, so he had arranged for protection in case things got out of hand. He checked his cellphone – with the text message ready to send – before entering the Major's office.

The Major was on the phone, chewing out a reporter, but his ire was turned on Richard and fury streaked from his barred teeth and bulging eyes as spittle shot like bottle rockets across his desk. His face grew purple as raw tuna flesh. Richard fingered the open scratches across his face and neck, checking for blood, feeling electric and alive, though he had barely slept in days, and he now stood in the office of a human being he despised. A human being who at this point surely had more hatred for Richard than he could ever imagine. Not a particular place to feel electric and alive, but the satchel at Richard's side held gold. His life was about to change. His time had arrived.

A crowd of employees had gathered outside of the Major's office. Richard Evans had been a wanted man since his colossal choke at Mann's Chinese Theater. The Major was so livid, so incensed, he had put a bounty out on the staff photographer. He wanted him alive, and he wanted him in person for the flaying. There was going to be hell to pay and a new policy for incompetence. The magazine had to license photographs from the event from a competitor. This cost the Major money and reputation. He'd been called by an executive at the parent company and suffered a humiliation that he was ready to turn on the pathetic sack of shit sitting across from him now, ready to pounce once this superfluous phone conversation ended. Mid-sentence, the Major simply slammed the phone down and called out to his secretary without taking his eyes of Richard.

"Get the paperwork on this dildo."

The secretary promptly produced a manila folder, which the Major opened with fat and raging fingers. "Close the fucking door," he told her as she exited.

Richards was alone with the Major in a closed room that was too hot and smelled of body odor and burnt sugar.

"This," the Major said, handing an official document to Richard, "is your termination notice. It was made effective on Tuesday evening at six o'clock. Right at the moment you failed to do what I pay you to do."

Richard looked at the document and fought the smile that was bouncing around his face, turning his lips into rubber.

"This," the Major seethed, "is a bill for the amount I had to pay to license photographs from the event which you failed to cover."

Richard looked at the document and choked a bit on the amount, though it only added to the figure he was holding in his head and was preparing to reveal. The beauty of this moment was not lost upon the young artist. Suddenly, every second he had struggled, every moment of desperation and doubt and shame, was validated, and this validation increased exponentially with every word the Major spoke.

"I realize you're a poor fucking loser," the Major said, contempt drooling all over his sentences, "and will always be a poor fucking loser, but you owe me that money. Your last paycheck has been withheld, and you are going to somehow come up with the rest in 60 days or I'm going to have your right arm ripped off and possibly shoved up your ass."

Richard sat up. The mirth had been drained out of him, and this moment took an unexpected turn as anger and exasperation spread through his cavity like dye. "Are you threatening me? I mean, like, really, truly physically threatening me?"

The Major jabbed a finger onto a pile of papers on his desk. "You're god damn right I am…" blathering on, doubling down on his angry promise, but Richard had tuned him out to reach inside his bag and do two things: send a text and retrieve a photo.

He fingered the fresh scratches on his face and neck as he held up a photograph that silenced the Major mid-sentence. His eyes bulged as his wet lips puckered repeatedly like a desperate fish. "Is that?"

"Yep," Richard said.

"And the broad?"

"Correct."

"And how did you get this?" he asked.

There was an element of genuine sincerity in the Major's voice, which was incongruous with his cynical nature. For a brief second, Richard tried to imagine him as a different animal.

"She has an estate way outside Santa Barbara, in the canyons past Neverland Ranch. I went up there yesterday and found the place after a few hours of searching. I crawled through the thick brush and took this shot from a ridge." He touched the scratches on his face and neck. "I had to climb a quarter mile to get that angle."

"Unbelievable," the Major muttered, his face flushed a soft shade of pink, his eyes fixed on the photo Richard proudly held just out of reach. "And who the hell told your sorry ass about their location?"

"A little birdie," Richard said with the flat stare of a seasoned spy just as Walter barged in the office and toppled the Major's desk, sending the owner of the furniture flying backwards to avoid being buried in splintered wood.

"The fuck are you," the Major screamed, sprawled on the floor, gripping his left shoulder as if experiencing the pains that preceded a heart attack.

The sudden violence had frightened Richard. Adrenaline surged through his body and his breath came in clumps. Still, he was able to comport himself to deliver a line straight out of Hollywood. "He's the little birdie I told you about."

With his teeth clenched and jaw wired, Walter seemed even more menacing as he stood hunched over the Major, ready to inflict more damage, like the henchman of a James Bond villain. The Major held up his arms like a frightened child.

"Call him off," the Major demanded. "Call him off!"

"Can't do that," Richard said, feeling empowered. "He doesn't work for me, just like I don't work for you." He held up the termination document.

"We can figure something out," the Major said, a thread of pleading weaved into his words.

"That's what I came to do," Richard said. "I'm an artist, not a publisher. I need someone to buy the rights to my work and do all the licensing, because this is big. Huge. Obviously, I don't care who does it, that's why I came to you, but that was before you threatened me."

Betrayal and payback freighted the last of Richard's words.

The Major made a keening sound, as if all the detritus of his corrupt life was piling up on its way to overwhelming his existence. People outside the door were gossiping, peeking through the window and laughing. Someone took a picture.

Richard stood up, still holding the photograph. "It even has a name – one that I'm sure a soulless scumbag like you can appreciate."

The Major raised his eyebrows, unable to hide his curiosity. Richard motioned for Walter to exit first, and on his way out, behind the giant battering ram who parted the crowd without lifting a finger, Richard turned his head back towards the Major and shared the name which perfectly encapsulated the photograph: "Martinis & Bikinis."

*

Walter and Richard drove in silence away from the offices of *Sellebrity Skin* magazine and up Wilshire Boulevard. The top was down in Walter's vehicle, the wind whipping in hot gusts across their faces, tangling their hair, as the sun began to scald their scalps and foreheads. Richard felt exhilarated and sick to his stomach. He kept replaying the events in the Major's office, wondering how he handled himself in the most dramatic confrontation of his life. It was his movie star moment, and despite the dramatic change of the expected script, he decided he had handled himself well. He was especially proud of the "little birdie" line. That was about as clever as he'd ever been. And then to have Walter barge in at that very moment! Magic. Art. But before Richard could enjoy his assessment, the reality that he now had other things to worry about dawned. He went to the Major because he wanted fast money and an easy outlet for the photo's distribution. As he drove away in the exposed auspices of Walter's jeep, he had neither.

"Can we put the top up?" Richard yelled through the roaring of the wind and the roaring of the Jeep's engine.

Walter shook his head. Richard used his hands to ask why. Walter shrugged and returned a sheepish grin.

"Super," Richard muttered as he slouched down in his hot seat, seeking some respite from the invasive elements and a swarming sense of desperation. He began to have doubts: about his talent and his plan and his agreeing to give 25% of the cut to Walter – a guy who drives around scorching Los Angeles with the top down.

Richard felt like giving up. He'd done what he was good at: snapped an exquisite photograph. Maybe the best he'd ever taken. All the other rigmarole associated with this plan was not his domain. The duplicity and the negotiating and the confrontation. He'd toughened up plenty since stepping off that bus from Fresno, but he didn't have the spine for all the high-stakes maneuvering that was now still required. He'd exhausted his ability for such interaction already. Showing up at Blue Roses and selling his idea to the angry Brit, the 24 hours in Santa Barbara, the confrontation with the Major, all of it left him limp. He was an artist, not a con-man or a tough guy or an executive. For the first time in ten years, Richards considered going back to Fresno.

Sensing Richard's consternation, and fearful of the bloke's thin skin, Walter whipped the Jeep into a drive that descended into a parking garage. The shade was a balm for Richard, who sat up and studied the hulking Brit who wore a mask of determination. "Got an idea," he muttered without moving his jaws.

After parking in a handicap spot near the entrance, Walter yanked out his cellphone and pushed a speed dial button, holding the phone cautiously away from his wired jowls.

"Mona," he muttered "What's that wanker's name, the one who works for the radio clown?"

Walter nodded and repeated the name delivered instantly to his ear. "Right. Jerry D. Right. Ring him, would you, and ask him if he'd interested in maybe the most glorious celebrity photo ever taken."

Richard knitted his eyebrows in curiosity. Walter hung up the phone and looked at Richard. "We should 'av done this right off."

"Done what?"

"Gone to Bernie Golden."

The two men sat silent in the cool of a covered parking garage. A minute later Walter's phone rang. "What he say?" was how he answered.

He listened for a few moments before speaking again. "Good. Tell him we'll be there in 30 and to have his checkbook handy."

Richard's viscera turned to ice water.

*

The open foyer of the gleaming office building in Burbank that housed the radio studio and corporate offices of Ramcin International was cool and quiet. It felt tense to Richard, like a library or a hospital. Few words were exchanged in the lobby as a Chinese receptionist at a security desk, in front of a giant corporate logo, greeted him and Walter with a nod and a mechanical smile before directing a serious Chinese security outfit to escort them upstairs.

Richard's heart pulsed and his pores tingled along his hair and neckline. His underarms felt icy. He clutched the satchel at his side and fought to keep his chin off his chest. Walter made slow marching movements next to him and breathed audibly through his nose. The security guards occasionally shot them sideways glances, but kept their eyes primarily on the digital numbers above the doors that indicated the escalating floors.

Richard felt a ping at his heart as a bell rang and the elevator car came to a stop. Jerry DeLaBomba, skinny arms and little legs, big round glasses balanced on a Roman nose, was waiting on the landing. He spread his arms and smiled at Walter.

"Mona tells me this is big," he said, his eyes alive with anticipation. "And if Mona says it's big, it's big."

"It's big," Walter confirmed, walking past the unusual man towards a rounded glass coffee flanked on two sides by leather couches along the far wall. Across the open area, along the opposite wall, was a table lined with a lunch buffet, glass bowls full of soft drinks floating in ice water, and a high-end coffer machine.

Walter motioned for Richard to sit down and promptly followed suit, securing a position between him and Jerry who had sat in the middle of the adjacent couch, leaning forward with his unusual arms draped across his narrow thighs. His eyes appeared to be banging into the lenses of his glasses. The open area was dimly lit and austere. There was no one else present. Down the long hall, lights of the radio studio flashed above the door and through the glass. Richard could sense the tension, like an open power channel, emanating from the room.

"Show him," Walter said to Richard.

With fumbling fingers, Richard unfastened his satchel bag and handed the photo to Jerry. When their hands met for the exchange, Walter locked his grip around Jerry's wrist.

"Try anything funny with this photo and your chicken neck will be snapped."

"Come on," Jerry said, offended and embarrassed and bristling with curiosity. Walter released his hold and Jerry slowly brought the picture to a position for study.

He adjusted his glasses. Studied it some more. "That's…:"

"Right," Walter said.

"And…"

"Correct," Walter added.

"Holy mother of God," Jerry said, standing up as if on command. "I gotta get Bernie."

Walter reclaimed the picture and handed it to Richard as Jerry Delabomba high-stepped away from the conference area and rushed down the long hallway towards the studio.

"Be sure to come back with your checkbook!" Walter yelled, as best he could, after him. He sat back and slapped a big hand hard across Richard's thigh. The pain felt good, and Richard felt his focus return, loaded with weapons he had amassed in his head on the ride over.

Walter got up and approached the lunch table. On a bagel, he made himself a heaping sandwich of lunch meats, topped with coleslaw with a pile of pickles on the side. He came back to join Richard with his lunch on a plastic plate held with both hands, a soda can stuck in his front pocket. He looked content, immersed in simple pleasure, until reality washed the joy from his face. Walter rattled the plate onto the table in front of him and rubbed his wired jaw.

"Bloody bastard," he mumbled, crossing his arms over his thick chest, eye-balling the photograph of Jack Flaherty that Richard balanced on his lap. Richard had no animosity towards Jack Flaherty, nor Angelica Lightman. In fact, he kind of admired the way they comported themselves as anti-celebrities, shunning the spotlight, unlike most of their craven contemporaries. It was rare and refreshing. But this was not about them. This was business, and Richard sat up quickly when he heard the tanic voice of Bernie Golden approaching down the hallway.

"This better be good, pulling me out of the studio during a show," he said over his shoulder toward the trailing Jerry, though he was clearly speaking to the two men on the couch who awaited his arrival. Bernie Golden walked fast, dressed in faded jeans and a wind breaker emblazoned with the name of a key sponsor. A tweed newsboy hat was turned backwards on his head, allowing tufts of auburn hair to curl along the brim like tendrils. "I'm live right now and have no time for any bullshit."

He stood in front of Richard and asked, "What do you got?"

Walter stood up and offered his hand. Bernie looked with contempt upon the gesture and lowered his eyes to Richard. "Well?"

Richard handed Bernie Golden the magical photograph. Walter's mouth began to move, but Bernie held up a hand as he kept his eyes locked on the photo. "I want this," he said, like a child mesmerized by a toy. "I'll take this."

"Ah," Jerry queried from a few feet behind Bernie. "How much we talking here?"

Walter's mouth began to move, but Richard held up a hand. "10 million," he said without pause or reservation.

Walter's head snapped as if he'd just been popped on the chin. Jerry peeled off a humorless laugh. Bernie Golden continued to stare at the photo he held a few inches from his face.

"You've gotta be fucking kidding me," Jerry said, in a negotiator's tone. "The broad is barely in the picture. The quality is average, at best."

The last part of the comment stung Richard a bit, but he knew it was all a game: the quality of the picture was extraordinary; so was the content. Everyone in the room knew it. He'd been thinking about this in a new light since the Major's reaction – how a cynical, soulless fuck with absolutely no taste at all had been rendered nearly silent by the photo and brought to the status of a whimpering child. He also remembered the envious gossip in the office about the ludicrous amounts paid to certain high-level celebrities for exclusive photos: babies, weddings, post-rehab or after significant weight loss. The ones that graced the cover of the higher-end celebrity magazines. The ones that choked the primary display spots of newsstand kiosks and were stuffed into tens of millions of mailboxes across America each week.

"Who owns this radio station?" Richard asked rhetorically to Jerry.

"Why?" he asked, suspicion freighting the tone.

"Just tell me."

"Ramcin International."

"And didn't Ramcin International pay $20 million for the pictures of those twins born last year?"

"Yeah, but those pictures were arranged, taken in a controlled environment by a real photographer."

Richard looked at Walter, who growled and causally removed the picture from Bernie Golden's slippery fingers. The infamous radio personality made a face like a little child and retreated towards the studio, nearly stomping his feet.

Richard kept his eyes on the producer, "And when the rapper married the reality show star…"

"Same deal," Jerry countered. "We're talking multiple photos, taken by a hired photographer, not a single shot snapped by some paparazzo hiding in the bushes." He made a point of passing his eyes over Richard's scratches, holding out his hands as if he were making perfect sense.

"That's why we're asking for less," Richard said, trying to keep a lid on the shrillness that was rising in his voice. "One picture – 10 million. And if you say another word about the quality of this photograph, I'm going home."

"OK, OK," Jerry said, pushing the glasses back up his nose. "Calm down. Calm down. I just can't agree to something like this. It'd be my ass." He looked up, towards the higher floors. "I gotta ask the Chinks."

"I understand." Richard said, coolness returning to his voice. "Do what you have to do. You have 30 minutes."

Jerry pursed his lips and nodded before disappearing down the hall. Walter burrowed his eyes into Richard, a look of absolute awe bouncing all over his face.

"Fuckin' A," he said, delivering a slap across Richard's shoulder that sent the skinny photographer onto the couch, where he leaned his head back and closed his eyes.

He couldn't believe what was happening. The figure he planned to offer the Major was one million, though he considered it extravagant and was more than willing to take a fraction of that amount. Among the swirling components of shock and elation was a sense of foreboding. He could feel it. Something sinister and craven. Something antithetical to his intention, and he could sense it begin to metastasize. Now it was out of his control; events would soon overwhelm and explode what Richard considered a grandiose intention from the beginning. He had no idea.

*

90 minutes later, Richard Evens, from Fresno, California, a lonely child of kind yet reticent parents, ten years struggling as an artist in near poverty and obscurity in Los Angeles, was a millionaire. Many times over. Fame, that fateful companion to West Coast wealth, was only a few minutes away. His skin buzzed; his feet tingled. His nostrils struggled to take in enough oxygen to keep him from tipping over. The consternation about his corrupted idea had been checked somewhere in the coat room of his conscience. A sense of the surreal shrouded him, as if he'd been graced by one of the Greek god's mists, making

him more than a mere mortal: taller, stronger, far more handsome. Comfortable. More than anything else, he just couldn't get over how easy it was. How mountains of money exchanged hands over a single photograph of two people. The sad reality and tragic portent still troubled Richard, but at the moment, he primarily felt nothing more than exultation after leaving the Ramcin International building and safely arriving at the office of Spence Berman, escorted by the Brit who had once broken his camera but now served as both a partner and protector.

Spence Berman was not there. After the angry episode a week earlier with Angelica Lightman and Jack Flaherty, one that had left him bleeding, deeply hurt and baffled beyond comprehension, he had left Los Angeles for a much needed escape to the remote outer islands of Hawaii. He did not indicate when he might return. Now, Richard Evans sat in Spence's chair, the city of Burbank rising, as if in tribute, behind him. Mona and Walter sat on the other side of Spence's desk. Walter looked at Richard with admiration, nodding affirmatively and shaking his head, spending the riches he amassed in his imagination. Mona talked incessantly, with clipped cadence, into her headphone, typing furiously into a laptop, arranging access to the newly established accounts where the large sums of money had been transferred. Without warning, pages were produced by a nearby printer.

Even fast at work, Mona noticed the time and quickly found a remote, from which she activated the flat screen on the far wall of the office. It turned on in an instant, already on one of the passel of celebrity channels operated by Ramcin International, the specific one that formerly aired time-delayed video footage of the Bernie Golden Show before the incident with Jack Flaherty that ended that practice and now simply aired the live audio from the show. The flat-screen in Spence's office held a still-frame of Bernie Golden, one of his regular print ads: the talk show host in headphones leaning towards a microphone, conducting his business sitting on a toilet seat with pants bunched around his ankles, as an audio recording of today's show was piped in. Mona abruptly ended her phone conversation and smiled at Richard. "Here we go," she said.

The three of them stared at the screen, though there was no motion there and the incongruous sound came from speakers stationed randomly around the office. Soon, they were surrounded by the live sound of the radio program.

"OK, people," Bernie Golden spoke in a low, ominous tone, the sound of his grinding teeth nearly audible over the air. "This is what I've been waiting for. The moment I have savored for my entire career, and never more so than the last few weeks, after that deviant, that disgusting specimen of celebrity, that speck of feces, dared challenge my authority. And not just my authority, *our* authority. We own this town. We own this country. We own these people whom we pay egregious amounts to shake their toned bottoms and mouth the words we pay them to speak. And when our authority was challenged, I put out a bounty on the head of the aggressor, and that bounty was brought in to me full fold, in merely a matter of weeks. I hold in my hand now a photograph. Though it is more than a photograph. It is the soul of the subjects, for it proclaims, without equivocation, that the subjects of this photo belong to us for as long as they feed at our trough. And for as long as they do so, they must know, as this picture proves, there is nowhere for them to run and nowhere for them to hide, and if they challenge our authority they shall be hunted and humiliated without exception and without mercy."

Silence followed Bernie's fervent and bizarre sermon to open the segment. The radio waves bristled until the silence was broken by the somewhat affected and gravelly voice of Leonard Temple. "Ah, well, thank you, Bernard, for that opening. My standard disclaimers about anything to do with the views of this program aside, I am honestly intrigued by this photograph and honored to have been asked to describe the imagery since it seems to say so much. Honestly, I've never seen anything quite like it, and I mean anywhere, not just in the realm of celebrity photography. The last 90 minutes around here have been quite frantic, as you can imagine, once this treasure entered our doors, and while Bernie used the time to pen his strange manifesto, I did some research on the photographer. His name is Richard Evans, and , not surprisingly, he is not your typical, hack paparazzo. He's an artist. He has an BFA from the University of Southern California. His eponymous website is a photo gallery of some of the most exquisite photographs I've ever seen. It is, quite simply, the story of Los Angeles."

Sitting in Spence's office, Richard's body was wracked by chills brought on by the words spoken on the radio. The familiarity of the voice only added freight to their meaning. He bowed his head and made a visor over his eyes with his hands, overwhelmed by the moment which was interrupted by the sound of Mona's fingers typing furiously into her laptop.

"Congratulations," she said. "Your website just crashed. I guess there's a buzz."

A cacophony erupted through the speakers, and disparate voices barked at Leonard to get on with it. "Fine," he said. "I shall use my narrative skills to describe what I hold, but I did feel compelled to recognize the artist behind what I believe is a masterpiece."

A full five seconds of silence followed before the narrative of Leonard Temple began in a theatrical voice:

"Imagine a late afternoon, a pale blue canvas in the distance, collecting the last remnants of light in the western sky. Consider a ridge, covered in cactus and sage and scrub brush. The arid domain of jackrabbits and rattlesnakes is sequestered from an oasis by a row of verdant cypress trees transplanted from more fecund earth. In the shaded oasis, a kidney-shaped pool shimmers as a figure emerges from the cool depths, rising from the water with straight arms pushing from the pool's lip, a lithe, olive-toned figure dripping water down a rippled torso with matted pubic hair exposed and the shaft of a penis just visible above the pool's edge. This, it appears, is the actor Jack Flaherty. A chaise lounge is angled on

the tiled surface surrounding the pool. A long, milky leg extends towards the water, a white bikini bottom gracing a slender hip. The upper torso is out of sight, but a tilted head of dangling blond tendrils frames a profile of a woman who resembles, almost undeniably, Angelica Lightman. Tucked at the hip of this beauty is a small table with a glass top, on it rests two martini glasses coated with frost, a clear pitcher filled with ice and translucent liquid. On the tabletop is also a straining device, a plate with speared green olives, and what appears to be the compliment to the bikini bottoms, draped lazily alongside the cocktail accoutrement.

After a moment of silence, Leonard broke from his narrative voice to mutter, "I've never wanted a drink so badly in my life."

Back in Spence's office, Mona turned off the program. "Well," she said. "That ought to help things quite a bit."

*

That evening, Mona, Walter, and Richard had a celebratory dinner at a Beverly Hills steak house owned by a chef and TV personality who spent nearly the entire evening walking the floor in a spotless uniform and ridiculous hat. Mona and Walter indulged, for starters, in bottles of Champagne and a seafood tower of oysters, shrimp, and lobster tails, while Richard sipped a cocktail of some sort clogged with muddled mint. He didn't like seafood, nor was he particularly hungry. His steak was under-cooked (the waiter ignoring his request for it to be cooked "medium"), and the wine overpriced ($500 for a 1997 Brunello di Montalcino that tasted, to Richard, like rusty raisin juice). The highlight of the evening was when a thoroughly sloshed Walter swirled his amber digestive out of its snifter and across the silk bosom of a nearly-as-inebriated Mona. When she dashed off for the bathroom, with a cackling and apologetic Walter stumbling after her, Richard folded his cloth napkin on the tabletop and left.

He climbed into his rusted Honda Civic and drove 150 miles in the middle of the night to his parent's home in Fresno where he slept for most of two straight days. On the third day, he took his mother and father to Best Buy and bought them a flatscreen TV and a desktop computer. They had no idea that their son had become an overnight millionaire, many times over, but they were pleased that he had some money in his pocket and had come home for a visit possessing a quiet confidence that he'd never had before. He stayed for a few days in the warm solitude of his parent's pastoral life. His clothes from high school still fit him, and it was nice to feel comfortable in items previously discarded. With his parents, he ate meals at local chain restaurants and saw a few movies. He accompanied his father to the shooting range. At home, they watched the local news while eating off of TV trays, sipping sweet tea. He sat in his old room a lot, listening to his favorite albums that were still stored in the milk crates the filled his closet. When it was time to leave, Richard got into his car and drove back to his apartment in LA.

The light and heat of Los Angeles seemed particularly intense as he exited the freeway and jockeyed down Wilshire Boulevard. It was mid-morning on a random weekday, but an intensity existed that gave Richard pause. He'd been avoiding media for the past week, which wasn't hard to do in his parent's house in Fresno, but in LA such an attempt felt futile as the shallow culture seemed to infuse the smoggy air. Still, Richard kept his car radio off and his eyes straight ahead, avoiding even a glimpse at passing newsstands and billboards.

He parked in the basement of his large apartment building and walked through the dim light of the garage, his soles echoing off the cold and open surface. The elevator was empty, as was the shadowed courtyard where his young professional neighbors often convened after work and on weekends. From the mailboxes in the arched hallway by the street-side entrance, in front of the gated-iron door, Richard retrieved a stack of mail from his jammed box. He walked the cement stairs to the 3ʳᵈ floor landing. A small dog barked behind a closed door as Richard stepped slowly to his studio apartment at the very end of the hall, his hands slightly shaking.

He turned his key slowly and eased open the door. The light revealed nothing unusual: the abbreviated hall that led to the small kitchen unit with a stove-top in the Formica counter, light streaming under the high-ceiling, into the hard-wood floor that held his mattress and desk and dresser. Through the sliding glass door in back, shadows of palm leaves swayed over the tiny deck with the knee-high hibachi and a single folding chair. The walls of the studio were bare and white plaster. The only sound was the humming of the half-refrigerator on the ground below a counter space and sink with two cupboards overhead.

As Richard drank some orange juice from the container, the light from the bathroom caught his eye as he dunked his head back to swallow. He left the container on the counter and walked slowly towards the bathroom with its door slightly ajar. He hadn't been home in over a week, not since his excursion to Santa Barbara, and the idea of the light being on frightened him immensely. Standing in his studio that random weekday morning, everything frightened him. He didn't feel safe, but he didn't know why.

Richard pushed opened the bathroom door and turned off the light. From the built-in closet next to the bathroom, he grabbed a backpack which he filled with clothes. He unplugged his knockoff laptop and secured it in a travel pack. From below the dresser, he retrieved his metal camera case, checked its contents, locked it back up with some valuable personal items secured from a secret desk drawer: passport, 9 mm handgun, tattered book of poetry, photograph.

With his personal items in hand, Richard returned to the parking lot where he got in his car and drove, once again, out of Los Angeles with his eyes straight ahead and the radio mute. This time, he went a few hours south to the coastal confines near San Diego where he checked into a suite with an ocean view under the iconic red turrets of the historic Hotel Del Coronado, where they had filmed *Some Like It Hot* with Marilyn Monroe in 1958, and the early aughts remake starring Angelica Lightman. Richard loved that movie, both versions, and always dreamed about visiting its location. Upon check-in, he asked the concierge to personally lock his metal camera case in the hotel's safe. Then he went to the boutique in the lobby and bought a bathing suit.

*

During Richard's retreat, much of America developed a singular obsession. The coverage of the photograph known as "Martinis & Bikinis" - introduced through the prose poetry of Leonard Temple on the Bernie Golden radio show - had erupted over the next week, appearing on over 100 magazine covers from pseudo-respectable celebrity weekly's to the daily rags which clogged the gutters of American media. On TV, it was the running feature throughout the programming of morning shows, evening celebrity programs and all day E-news outlets. And, of course, The Bernie Golden Show, claiming domain over the scandal and achieving a ratings boost to validate such claims, failed to recognize even another single subject for one week straight. The host himself had reached such a level of absurd imperiousness that he abandoned his namesake ritual at the beginning of the show and dedicated the entire opening segment to accrued evidence of his stature as the King of Media.

The entertainment industry fury was followed by front page stories in major newspapers about the exposure. Meta-stories appeared in national magazines, featuring the photo on their covers promoting articles contemplating the meaning of it all. It was considered by intellectuals as everything from the Zeitgeist to the end of art to the rebirth of American culture. *The New York Times* editorial board declared the picture "disturbing in its ability to distract national attention from more pressing matters, yet a work of art worthy of aesthetic recognition and public consideration." Nearly everyone had an opinion, from late night talk show hosts to popular athletes. The President of the United States was asked his opinion of the photograph at the end of a rare press briefing.

The Killing Kind became America's top movie despite not being a remake from the 80s or a part of a series based on fantasy novels for tweens, nor cartoon characters come alive, nor was it an outlandish buddy movie full of bathroom humor or a super-violent action film featuring superheroes or super-humans engaged in blood sport. Even more surprising was the correlation of box office success and solid reviews from the small band of serious critics who deemed the film "important" and "a serious-minded look at both domestic violence and the effects of foreign wars on our homeland." Footage of lines outside of theaters emerged from every corner of the country. The public fascination was not with the film's themes or storyline, but a portentous sex scene between the characters played by Mina Garcia and Jack Flaherty, where the violence lurking in the soldier recently returned from the Gulf wars played by Mr. Flaherty is obliquely revealed through vigorous, even combative, love making. The scene lasts an unusually long 15 minutes and was shot from various angles with maximum exposure, intimacy and intensity. It took three days to film and had to be edited for a week to allow for an NC-17 rating. There were frequent altercations within the theaters when moviegoers refused to give up their seats for the following showings.

A melee erupted in a New Jersey palladium and an ironic fire was set by angry viewers when a St. Louis multiplex was shut down by the fire department for overcrowding. Scalping of tickets and security became the norm outside of theaters. Midnight showings, complete with cocktails, were the rage.

The Martinis & Bikinis name was appropriated. There was a clever t-shirt with large boobs drawn as an M and a B, respectively, with an ampersand wedged into the cleavage. The original Martinis & Bikinis lounge opened, seemingly overnight, in Miami, complete with an indoor pool, bikini rentals and a martini menu. Similar franchises were planned in Las Vegas, Nashville, and Seattle. There was a FROYO flavor and a popular new vodka brand. The classic straight-up martini with olives experienced a renaissance, and the multi-martini lunch was once again in vogue despite the increase in DUI incidents and lower productivity in the work place.

The gossip machine raged on for weeks, most of it centered on the Bernie Golden Show, where the host had begun wearing cardigan sweaters, donning reading glasses and comporting himself like a pseudo-journalist. The lewd hi-jinx of the show had been replaced by a patina of seriousness. There were no "Golden" showers. Leonard Temple conducted the interviews in a respectable, insightful and, often, humorous fashion while the host sat silently for the most part, taking notes, only interrupting on occasion to ask pointed questions seeking flesh. The rest of the KBAL Crew were essentially rendered silent. The FCC fines reached record lows; ratings and revenue continued to climb.

Experts were brought in to attest to the identity of Angelica Lightman in the photograph. Others were brought in, based on the tantalizing yet limited exposure in the photo, to estimate the actual length of Jack Flaherty's penis. Old girlfriends, some real, some not, were dug up to offer expert authentication of all claims. All of the exes, real or not, despite steady prodding from the host to indicate the contrary, spoke of Jack as an excellent lover and a stand-up guy devoid of any serious flaws or fetishes.

Finally some dirt arrived in the form of a pretty and blond former-cheerleader from USC who claimed that Jack had sexual assaulted her at a post-game party, attempting to insert his penis in her ear, which caused some commotion for a few minutes until it was revealed, rather easily via the iPad Classic at Leonard Temple's disposal, that the woman making the claims was neither a former cheerleader at USC nor even a student at any time at the university (or any university). So, while the ear-fetish controversy failed to inspire any new narratives, the USC reference led to an assessment of Jack's gridiron accomplishments, which only added to the mounting mystique, and brought big Sid Fortunato and Smoov into the dialog, if only for a minute.

"We went back and watched the films of his two starts at SC," Sid said.

"And I gotta admit, guy had a cannon."

"Agreed," said Smoov.

"And composure in the pocket."

"Agreed, again, mang."

"We're looking at a serious athlete here, boss."

"Mmmm, hmmm. Is true."

"Shut up! Both of ya!" Bernie barked, showing his teeth for the first time in weeks, a sign that the narrative was moving away from his intended direction.

Meanwhile, the actual subjects of public fascination were absent from any participation whatsoever. Their whereabouts were unknown. The gutter rags ran rumors about breakups or belly bumps or sightings around the globe, all with the credibility associated with reports of UFOs, sea monsters or Sasquatch. In the same week they were spotted outside Cafe Du Monde in New Orleans, washing down beignets with coffee and warm milk, while also, reportedly, walking arm in arm in the Florentine twilight, while also shopping at a rug bazaar in Tunisia (he wore a fez; she cradled a domesticated monkey in her arm). Someone said they were in Kenya, adopting an entire village. Despite the obvious illegitimacy and geographic impossibility of the sightings, the magazines were consumed like crumbs of exquisite pastry until the slow fade began and other narratives began to bloom in the public conscious.

An American embassy in the Middle East had been attacked and 12 diplomats were killed. An armed, white supremacist from Mississippi was shot down on the streets of San Francisco. A bridge collapsed in Maine. An aging actress turned weight-fluctuation artist died of coronary arrest during the filming of a reality show documenting her latest attempt at weight loss (the cameras kept rolling as she held her chest and writhed on the kitchen floor). The Chicago White Sox won the World Series.

*

And it was among this backdrop of fading focus on the story of "Martinis & Bikinis" that the photographer Richard Evans paid a surprise visit to the studio of The Bernie Golden Show for a live interview. Richard arrived looking tan and well-rested. He wore a crisp white dress shirt, opened at the collar and untucked over skinny jeans and vintage Capezios. A faded canvas satchel was strapped across his chest.

Jerry DeLaBomba ferried him into the studio during a commercial break rapidly promoting the crew's professionalism while complaining vociferously about the call he just got from Mona announcing Richard's presence in the lobby. Jerry brought Richard to the table in middle of the room set up for Leonard Temple's interviews. He made the hasty introductions and bolted for the door.

"My, my, Jerry," Leonard purred, reclining back in a leather office chair, staring at the stranger before him, a finger petting his cleft chin. "You've finally brought me a man who looks like a little boy. And he's an artist to boot."

Richard shook Leonard's hand and then sat down in the leather chair next to him. The room smelled of coffee and lunch meat. The lights were low, but Richard was aware of the hard stare coming from Bernie Golden, sitting on his throne in his platform at the head of the room surrounded by plexiglass. He also heard the stilted bickering of Sid and Smoov behind him. Richard, as planned, kept his attention on Leonard. "That was an amazing description of the photograph. Thank you for that."

"Well," Leonard said, making a puckish face, "I was a poet once."

"I know," Richard said, pulling the tattered book of poetry from his satchel and showing it to Leonard. "I've read it 100 times."

Leonard took a copy of his own book and studied it as if he were seeing it for the first time. He looked at Richard with his mouth making an "O" shape inspired by wonder while his eyes squinted with lustful currency. "I'd be blushing right now, darling, if there was any blood above my waistline."

Richard blinked back his shock, absorbed the wallop of flattery and sudden attraction. He managed a subtle smile just as Jerry came in to count down seconds to air time. The room fell silent. Leonard swiftly fastened his headphones in place and handed Richard his own before straightening his posture and approaching the microphone mounted on the table in front of him.

"Well, well, Angelinos and other Americanos, just when we thought it was safe to get back in the proverbial water of normalcy, when we thought, well, at least most of us thought, do I dare say hoped, that the Martinis & Bikinis saga was finally ready to be put to bed, into the studio of The Bernie Golden Show strolls this tall glass of artistic insouciance, the man behind the photograph itself, Richard Evans. Welcome."

Richard hunched and loomed over his microphone. His heart felt like a nervous hamster stuck inside his chest cavity. "Ah," he quivered as his head spun. "Thank you."

With theateric coaching motions, Leonard got Richard to improve his posture and address the microphone appropriately. When Richard was in proper position, Leonard gave him a warm wink and encouraged him to breath.

"So, before what we begin what will surely be a rather informative discussion about this masterpiece of a photograph, I've been wondering all along about the title. Where did it come from?"

Richard took a deep breath and fought the urge to hunch. "It's the name of an album by Sam Philips. She's a singer from..."

"I knew it!" Leonard declared.

"You know her?"

"Do I? I gave the album a rave review in *Spin*."

"I think I spent most of my high school years listening to it, and a couple of other records, in my bedroom."

"Name another!" Leonard asked in the imperative, a jauntiness in his tone.

"*Girlfriend* by Matthew Sweet."

"I'm in love," Leonard sighed, an affected wrist draped across his forehead.

The studio was filled with a sense of romance and good will; the foreign presence alarming to the regular inhabitants. "Wait a minute. Wait a minute," Big Sid Fortunato interrupted, hulking over his microphone from his position directly behind the interview table. "You're saying you stole that title, from someone's, what, album? Isn't that plagiarism or something?"

The inability to answer the question, or even where to begin, caused Richard to blink repeatedly and swipe at his bangs as Leonard snapped his head sideways, leaned into the microphone and answered the question venomously with his profile turned to Sid.

"Absolutely not, you imbecile."

"How come?"

"Because artists borrow from other artists. It's part of the process."

"Sounds like stealing," Sid said, feeling the rare rush of intellectual empowerment.

"Yeah, mang," Smoov chimed in. "This dude need to be locked up."

Leonard took a deep breath and responded in a monotone, directly facing the microphone. "The appropriation of art by other artists is not stealing, it is inspiration. Artists feed each other's ideas. The more they expose themselves to the creations of others, the more creative they become as a result. It is an essential part of the process. My goodness, look at Bob Dylan, the man has been what you call 'stealing' for over 50 years, but no one dares refer to him as a thief."

"Bob Dylan," Smoov echoed. "Ain't he, like, dead?"

"This," Leonard droned. "Is precisely what's wrong with America."

"And what's that?" Big Sid asked, gleefully playing the foil.

"An absolute ambivalence for art."

"Art. Fart," Smoov giggled.

"Exactly," Leonard sighed. "Art. Fart. It's why our politics are joke and the polar caps are nearly gone and American school children are among the dumbest in the advanced world."

"Wow," Sid said. "Maybe we should go to a museum or something. You know, save the polar bears while we're at it."

"Yes, Sidney. Go to a museum. They have discounted rates for the new species known as Homo-Ignoramus."

"You call me a homo, Lenny?" Sid was serious.

"The point is that what this young man has done is an extraordinary accomplishment. He's created a work of art that has caused a sensation, no small feat in our day and age defined by the lowest common denominator, and in doing so he has been true to his times in the most profound way. And that is the job of the artist: to be true to the times in which they live. And the fact that he has chosen to name his creation after another work of art that came before and did not receive the appropriate consideration, well, that's just a nice twist of tribute on this already exquisite cocktail."

Sid and Smoov jabbered nonsensically. Richard wiped his hands on his thighs and caught Leonard's eye. The two men held their stare until Bernie Golden erupted from his throne.

"Enough!

The room went silent. Leonard rolled his eyes, sighed and removed his headphones, crossing his arms as he leaned back in his chair. Jerry DeLaBomba slipped into the room, his face covered in concern as Bernie seethed into his microphone.

"This is not a forum to debate the irrelevance of art, nor is it some queer dating show. I assume this guy is here for some reason relevant to *my* show. But before we get to that, before we get to the reason this person has come in here unannounced and uninvited, I have to ask him a question."

Leonard put his headphones back on. Richard leaned towards the microphone.

"Yes?"

Bernie pawed his own chin and eye-balled Richard. Speaking slowly in a menacing tone he asked, "Are you enjoying my money?"

"What?"

"My money. Are you putting it to good use?"

"I'm sorry," Leonard interjected. "Was your name on the check? I don't believe it was."

"Doesn't matter," Bernie struck back. "I made that money for the Chinks in the first place, and then I made them even more on the royalties it generated."

"Whatever you say," Leonard waxed sarcastic.

"Exactly, Lenny," Bernie responded. "Whatever I say, but your new friend hasn't answered my question."

"Ah, I'm sorry," Richard peeped. "What was the question?"

"Are. You. Enjoying. My. Money."

Richard shot Leonard a sly look and then addressed his microphone with an earnest expression. "Yes," he said. "I bought my parents a new TV and a computer."

"Beautiful," Bernie said. "That's all I wanted to know. Now tell me, what in the fuck are you doing here?"

The cash register rang and Jerry motioned frantically with his hands for the control booth to hit the delay button.

"Well," Richard said slowly, "considering how helpful you were with the promotion of the first photograph, I thought it would be appropriate for me to announce here, on your show, that there's more."

"Say it ain't so, lover," Leonard moaned, rubbing a palm into his eye socket.

Richard mouthed "Sorry" to him.

Leonard returned a playful smirk. Sid and Smoov took up their bantering until Bernie cut them off.

"Quiet. Quiet. Quiet. Quiet. Quiet. Quiet. Quiet. Quiet. Quiet."

He got his wish.

"Let me get this straight," Bernie said to Richard. "You have other pics? Of those two?"

"Yep."

"Taken when?"

"Same day."

"How many?"

"Lots. But only two worthy of publication."

"Get out."

"Out."

"Let me see them."

"No."

"Why not? Aren't they for sale? They gotta be for sale. Why else would you be here if you weren't after more of my money?"

"I hear that," Sid chimed in.

"Shut up," Bernie ordered. "I'm talking to the pho-tag. I don't want to hear any other voices. So, are they for sale or not?"

"Sort of."

"What's that mean?'

"They're for auction."

"Auction?"

"That's correct. The pictures go to the highest bidder." Richard looked at his watch. "The rules and method for bidding went live are on my website 10 minutes ago."

Mona had assured Richard she's secured a server that could handle all the hits, and he took solace in her competence. He looked Bernie Golden in the eye.

"Get the fuck out of here," Bernie spat.

The cash register dinged.

"Well, there's less money to offer now," Leonard joked.

"We got all the money we need," Bernie said, sounding definitive. "Let's just skip the charade and get this over with. Show me the pictures and I'll send Froggy upstairs for a check, same as last time times two. If there any good. Let me see them."

"Can't do that," Richard said.

"Fuck you mean, can't do that?"

"Chuk. Ding," went the register.

Richard cleared his throat and adjusted his posture. "I want America to use its imagination for a while."

Smoov hit the "Boooooinnng" button.

Richard was nonplussed. "I want America to be creative, to be challenged to think about something, about the possibilities of something potentially fantastic, as opposed to being spoon fed everything all the time."

"You're out of your mind," Bernie declared with a dismissive wave of his hand. "Get lost."

"What a joke," Sid said.

Richard stood up and secured his satchel. Just as it appeared he was going to leave he leaned down towards the microphone.

"The winner of the auction will own the rights to the photos. All of the proceeds from the winning bid, as well as 25% of all subsequent royalties earned, will go to fund arts in the Los Angeles public schools. All the details and entry information for the auction are on my website: www.richardevansartist.com. Again, I want America to use its imagination for a while. The dates for the auction are open ended. I will tell you this: The photos absolutely feature Jack Flaherty and Angelica Lightman. They are taken the same day I took "Martinis & Bikinis." In one picture the couple are dressed; and in the other there is complete nudity."

And with that, Richard made his exit.

"Bravo!" Leonard declared, standing up to offer applause. "Bravo."

*

Richard left the offices and walked the three blocks to where he had parked on a side street of W. Victory Boulevard. Blinding traffic zipped back and forth. The mid-afternoon sun seared his exposed skin and caused him to perspire beneath his clothes. His feet felt slippery within their socks when he reached his car, parked beside a small garden where hummingbirds clustered and chirped in a lipstick-red Azalea patch.

Richard felt elated and exhausted. Unsure if this aspect of their project would work, but thrilled about how things went on the radio show. Part of him wanted the whole thing to be over; part of him wanted it to continue indefinitely since the excitement somewhat appealed to him on both a visceral and spiritual level. Plus, he was meeting such interesting people.

Leonard Temple had been a hero of sorts to Richard while growing up. His brazen poetry about LA street life inspired Richard, as did his open sexuality and insightful reviews in credible rock journals. Leonard became a beacon of aesthetic for Richard, someone whose opinion informed his own even on things he had yet to be exposed. Richard had been deceitful in the studio. He had known that Leonard Temple reviewed Sam Philips' album *Martinis & Bikinis* in Spin magazine. He had read it in his room. That's why he bought the album, one that would not disappoint. Richard considered the album a masterpiece of atmosphere, hooks, and themes. It seemed almost dystopian to him, of some somber, futuristic time and place, but clearly inspired by the past. He conjured images to accompany the songs, and eventually created a narrative of still life photos based on the soundtrack that would serve as training for his creativity.

As lost as Richard became in the album, he did not lose track of the person who introduced him to it, a person, until the review in *Spin*, unbeknownst to him. Richard researched Leonard Temple and found him fascinating: a punk poet with brains and gay bravado. The son of B-actors, Leonard was Los Angeles born and raised. He attended Hollywood High School and dabbled in various arts and street life. As a teen, he haunted the rock clubs on the Sunset Strip and served as an unofficial A&R scout for Geffen Records. He openly claimed to have discovered Guns & Roses and also claimed to have co-written "Paradise City" in a Benzedrine frenzy with Axl Rose in a West Hollywood flop house.

Leonard's first book of poetry was well-received by critics, earning him fellowships and grants. His second collection won the Pushcart Prize, which led him to a career in music journalism and eventually the role of snarky (and often inebriated) self-proclaimed "Protector of Aesthetic" as one of three panelist on a wildly popular musical talent show for amateurs where he would infamously destroy wide-eyes wannabes with comments along the lines of: "I'm sorry, Darling, but as the Protector of Aesthetic, I must tell you that was atrocious. Go home and practice. Every day. Come back in seven years."

His most infamous moment was in the heat of a spirited debate with his rival panelist, a hip-hop diva of undetermined talent and ample attitude, whom Leonard told on a live season finale to "Suck my pussy, bitch." The phrase became a popular Twitter hashtag, a social media acronym (smp), and a pop culture meme, gracing everything from t-shits to cocktail napkins, a portend for Leonard's career.

And in the subsequent years, Leonard's excessive drinking led him to be fired and rehired numerous times, often too much fanfare among the legions of amateur music talent program fans who adored watching his snarky resurgence then slow spiral back down to the gutter of excess and humiliation (of himself and others). And eventually, after hitting rock bottom for the 5th time, going out in a blaze of glory, atop the panelist's table, ranting about the end of art as we know it, warning of a looming apocalypse and the end of the American empire, Leonard ended up on *Celebrity Rehab*, where he shared a Malibu house with, among other degenerates, an actress and future senator from West Virginia, a cup cake mogul, a Pittsburgh Steelers' quarterback, and the once highest-paid sitcom actor in America. After successfully completing the program, Leonard was hired by the fledgling Bernie Golden Show to be the master of ceremonies in the self-proclaimed "Humiliation Theater" and foil to the host and his bombastic crew, a position Leonard openly loathed and admitted only doing for the much-needed money.

Richard had lost track of Leonard Temple over the years, subconsciously ignoring his public disgrace, and was more than pleasantly surprised to rediscover his presence in the "Martins & Bikinis" adventure. He suspected that Leonard might be an unwitting ally, which he had been to a great extent; he never suspected that he would be more than that. Richard turned on his car radio and listened to the show, Leonard's voice fluttering in his heart like the hummingbirds beating their wings in the Azalea patch. The stakes for Richard in this whole affair had somehow been raised.

*

Jack's cousin Jeannie powered off her cellphone and cursed under her breath. She was alone backstage at a campus theater in Charlottesville, VA. She'd been trying to reach Jack for weeks, but he had disappeared without a word at the onset of "Martinis & Bikinis." She had no idea where he was or any clue as how to find out. She figured he and Angelica, if there were even still together, had escaped somewhere exotic, though it was just as likely, knowing Jack, that the publicity had offended his sensibilities and inspired a singular flee to some remote corner of New England. She, from a very young age, had admired Jack's independence, but now she hated him for his bouts of recluse behavior, especially when she needed him so desperately.

The band had been booked on a tour up and down the eastern seaboard, playing mid-sized venues in mid-sized cities, as well as auditoriums on college campuses, where they did radio interviews on college stations, the last avenue of exposure on the airwaves for new music acts. The events were well attended, and the band was being courted by various independent distribution consortia, which was the best thing a new band could hope for in the current state of the record "industry." It was all very validating to Jeannie, after so many years of struggle for attention, but the recent acclaim had been troubling to her as well.

She worried that the new-found notoriety Jezebel received was due primarily to their association with Jack and Angelica. It all came on the heels of the t-shirt stunt in Boston. There is no doubt about the correlation, but the adulation, especially from college radio programmers, was real. And they had earned it though perseverance and dedication to an aesthetic that continued to expand. There was clearly a contingent of pathetic gawkers and amateur paparazzi at their shows, drawn by the sensational and the chase of celebrity, but enough of the crowd - a clear majority - came for the music. Jeannie could feel their energy on stage. She could hear them sing along and react to the openings of certain songs. Jezebel was building an informed and dedicated audience. This was enormously validating to Jeannie, though it was all belied by the recurring presence of one particular fan.

The soldier from the Boston gig - the handsome and damaged one - the one recently back from the Gulf Wars and unaware of irony - had shown up in Philadelphia and Baltimore and DC. Jeannie had spotted him standing alone in the crowd, in jeans and a t-shirt. It was easy to do. He stood ramrod straight near the front of the stage and didn't take his eyes off of her, moving ever so slightly to the music. She'd ignored him and never mentioned his presence to the band. He never tried to contact her before or after the shows, nor reach her through the band's Social Media avenues. It struck Jeannie as somewhat romantic yet scary, too. She hated feeling scared, and wanted someone to protect her. Her father knew some people, but he'd bought a place on the Amalfi coast after selling the restaurant to D'Antonio for more than he'd ever imagined. She didn't want to bother her father overseas or cause him any undue worry. She wanted Jack to be there for her, like he'd always been. But he was nowhere to be found in the aftermath of "Martinis & Bikinis."

And now Jeannie was alone, far from home and ambivalent about her band's success, wondering if the handsome and damaged soldier would be waiting for her in a few moments when she took the stage.

*

Walter snored in Mona's bed. He'd been into his cups, as usual of late, and awake when she came home, but he'd fallen into a sleep apnea riddled stupor before she could even freshen up in the bathroom and change into her silky canary camisole. She'd been out in Century City with her acquaintance from Northwestern University, Susan Levine, who came to LA to write screenplays or TV scripts, which she did unsuccessfully while living off her father's largess, and had somehow found great success acquiring original programming for the premium cable channels. She'd rejected six of Mona's previous treatments/ideas, but still enthusiastically accepted her invitations to dinner.

They met in a dimly-lit Viennese bistro designed as a speakeasy that was accessed through a faux-pharmacy on a side street. It had become chic in LA to pay homage to prohibition in anticipation of its 100th anniversary, though the real roaring in the years approaching 2020 was done by the sun. Due to the heat, 11:00 PM had become the new 9:00, the normal time for a casual dinner, trendy restaurants first seating, in the hours after the asphalt had been slightly cooled by the ocean breezes that nudged some of the smog over the mountains.

Susan sat at the mahogany bar, sipping an Acai Berry Martini in the dim light. She greeted Mona with kisses on each cheek. The women expertly exchanged compliments about outfits and appearances. The collective of private conversations created a cacophony beneath the low and tin ceiling, but it was still early enough to get a table. They were seated at a corner two-spot by a hipster Maitre'd in suspenders and rolled-up sleeves, his hair slicked down the middle and a tattoo-handlebar mustache and muttonchops expertly-inked in the space a traditional facial hair would cover.

Mona ordered a straight-up dirty Martini with three olives. The women made small talk for a few minutes before Susan got down to the business, she assumed, was at hand.

"So, what are we working on?"

Mona shrugged, sipped her drink and confessed to having nothing to offer. She just wanted a dinner with a friend, no agenda. Susan studied Mona for a moment and then broke into the type of genuine smile that she hadn't made in years.

"Really?"

"Really."

The two women drank cocktails and ate soy schnitzel. They reminisced about college and their early days in LA. The industry came up, and they spoke openly about players with whom they were both familiar. Still, it was seemingly as genuine a conversation either woman had had in ages - they laughed easily and reached across the table to touch each other after particularly salient or salacious thoughts were shared - though Mona's participation was decidedly disingenuous. She did have an agenda. Really. She knew the cache of Martinis & Bikinis among the elite had worn off in the weeks after the original photo had been released. What she wanted to find out from Susan Levine, a bonafide barometer of LA's upper-crust wisdom, was if the auction for the second set of photos had recaptured the attention of those with power in the industry. Mona wanted their acceptance, and knew this was her way in or out, depending on the buzz.

At home in her bungalow in the hollows of Pacific Palisades, Mona climbed into bed next to the slumbering Walter and powered on her vintage iMac. It was slow, but lovely and a cherished gift from Spence. She thought of his exile in Hawaii and felt guilty about manipulating him as she had. He had been good to her over the years. Taking her on as a client when she was young and new to LA. Getting her the forgettable roles in major motion pictures and many supporting roles in the short-lived B-movie renaissance of the 21st century, mostly horror movies where Mona was the BFF of the leading lady, either the first or the last victim of recurring or original psycho-killers, experiencing death in myriad ways, always exposing herself at frequent intervals before being covered in fake blood in the end, for hours at a time during grueling and often humiliating days on a makeshift set. And when the humiliation had become too much, and the roles no longer attainable, Spence had taken her on as his assistant after she had, over the course of a few years, convinced him of her acumen for the entertainment industry.

She was certain that she could reinvent Spence in a way that would extend his significance well into the 21st century. He had taken her advice and began an independent production company, but he brought Angelica Lightman in on it and let her have almost all of the control. Mona had no problem with Angelica, and even admired her career as an actress and noble attempt at anonymity, but she was inaccessible to Mona - as she was to nearly everyone - so she had to do her bidding through Spence. Mona had submitted eight original treatments, some of which, if not all, she was certain could acquire Angelica's approval if Spence had bothered to show her; instead, he filed them in his drawer where Mona found them one day - the day she began plotting.

That was when she turned to Walter, the burly and cocky Brit, valet/bodyguard of Angelica Lightman, who had squeezed her ass at a recent cocktail party and appeared in the office on occasion, ferrying items between Angelica and Spencer. She promptly seduced him, began an affair, and convinced him to present Angelica with the script she had written called *The Killing Kind*. It was submitted under a pseudonym, and Mona had the unique experience, after its acceptance by Spence and Angelica's production company, of contacting herself via e-mail - on behalf of their nascent and anonymous film company, to make an offer on the rights to a screenplay she had written, and then - after a brief negotiation - she prepared the contract rights and cut a nice-sized check, all made out to her secret self.

Walter shot up from his sleep. His breathing seized and he pushed off the mattress, holding the pose for a few seconds, before returning to his groaning slumber. Mona was used to Walter's drunken-apnia. At first it had terrified her, certain - as she was - that he was having a heart attack in his sleep. He was impossible to rouse yet clearly alive as evidenced by the snoring. She found Walter simple yet charming in his utterly unique way, and they had fallen into a nice routine. He was her younger stud who brought much needed companionship and an awakening of her dormant sex life. He also brought her secret access to Spence and Angelica's film company and the production of her first screenplay. And all of this largess was meager compared to the real prize Walter had brought to Mona: Richard Evans and his idea that would become "Martinis & Bikinis."

From her iMac, Mona accessed Richard's website. She'd been ignoring it for a few days, staying removed from the auction results, partly to remain pragmatic and partly to avoid the potential of its failure. She didn't like the auction idea; but they had insisted, so she went along. Now Susan Levine had dashed Mona's fears and validated her deepest wishes: The industry's elite were abuzz with the auction. It was considered high-brow. And while none of the remaining elite money was gauche enough to participate in the event, it was followed with courteous detachment that belied a carnal fascination - kind of like how the wealthy and non-threatened watch blood sport.

Mona was certain that Susan's reveal validated her involvement in the project, if not its mastermind, certainly the brains behind its actuation. With shaking hands she punched in passwords and navigated the website's secret pages. The bidding - anonymous to the public - had reached staggering heights. There were a few wealthy individuals - Russian oligarchs, American hotel heiresses, and popular business moguls - but the real money came from media corporations. And topping the list was Ramcin International.

*

Bernie Grossman had remained aloof to the auction at first. He was offended by that limp-wristed paparazzo grandstanding on his show, flirting with his minion. And his show was not a vehicle for self-promotion. Especially for those who have the audacity to still consider themselves artists in modern America. Bernie declared the whole auction a joke and, moreover, a pathetic attempt at art. A disgrace. He went on a two-day rant: Richard Evans was a one-hit wonder who was desperately trying to extend his 15 minutes of fame that Bernie had permitted in the first place. This proved once and for all that the media ruled and artists were simply their servants who should be grateful for any attention they get, but that attention is doled out by the media, not to be dictated by so-called artists, who were figments of their own imagination. Art was dead. Entertainment, in any form, was what mattered. Art did not. We were a nation of frogs, hopping from fad to fad with nothing deeper to be gleaned along the way than meager distraction from our miserable everyday lives.

Richard's efforts and auction had offended Bernie Golden's sense of order, his entire professional philosophy, which he had built into nothing short of an empire. His ratings were the highest in the nation. The advertising rates on his show had reached record amounts. Numbers did not lie. He was the king of the world. And it was up to him to decide when the respective runs of each and every fad would end. Richard Evans' appearance on his show and his announcement of that absurd auction was, from Bernie's point of view, a betrayal. The farce of an auction was an offence, and attention to said offence would belie the very foundations of which his kingdom was built. The king declared the fad officially over.

But the fad wouldn't die. *The Killing Kind* kept drawing crowds and "Martinis & Bikinis" continued to appear on newsstands and homepages. Many of the conversations went beyond the sensational and focused on more insightful aspects of each offering. There was a buzz about the Oscars for the first time in years. The auction started slowly but was soon bolstered by attention-seeking individuals with money to burn. Speculating on the images in the photo became fever sport. Entries flooded in for the contest. Word came to Jerry DeLaBomba from upstairs: They wanted in. So Bernie Golden acquiesced and turned his attention back to the narrative he had himself declared a farce. His narcissism allowed this convenient contradiction, and he spoke of the scenario as if he had been pulling the strings all along. He explained it to the nation with a God-like reverence for himself:

His obsession with Angelica Lightman and his subsequent beef with Jack Flaherty had brought them together. In doing so, he had delivered America its most delicious fad. And the end result would be the ultimate humiliation of those who dare ignore or challenge him. A fatal blow to anyone who challenged the new paradigm. This had been his plan all along. He had moved mountains to make it happen. And now it was bigger than him; it was bigger than media; it was the new America.

He dramatically dispatched Jerry upstairs to tell the Chinks he wanted a blank check.

"My, my," Leonard Temple quipped. "Da-Nile ain't just a river in Egypt, baby."

*

Mona choked when she saw the amount from Ramcin International. It was twice the previous leading bid. She stared at the computer screen for an hour. The contest was over. It was time to get Richard to pick three winners and to get his ass back up to Los Angeles.

*

Richard held the wheel of his Civic with one hand; his other hand rested atop the metal brief case retrieved from the concierge at the Hotel Del Coronado and now strapped into the passenger seat beside him. He had checked to make sure the contents were undisturbed before checking out of the hotel. He wore a sear sucker suit with a silk undershirt, leather sandals and aviator sunglasses. All of his other belongings were left in the room, and he journeyed alone on Highway 5 along the coast from San Diego towards Los Angeles, his right hand firmly atop the metal case and its precious belongings.

Just past noon, Richard veered off the highway and into the drive-thru at In & Out Burger. In the parking lot, Richard ate the juicy sandwich and salty fries with the reverence of a last meal, before returning to the road as the highway moved inland. As the Civic traveled north, Richard sucked the last drops of soda from the wax-sealed cup before removing the plastic cap to access the ice chips, which he methodically crunched between his molars as the barren suburban scenery of Orange County flashed past and the anxiety rose through his sternum as he approached the bloated belly of smog-choked Los Angeles.

The shift from highway cruising to city jostling unsettled Richard even more, but he kept a steady gaze through the front windshield as he navigated the crowded afternoon streets of weekday Los Angeles before passing a glistening tower on W. Victory Boulevard in Burbank. He drove a few blocks further and then parked on a side street in front of an Azalea patch teeming with hummingbirds. He waited in the car until a one word message - "Done" - appeared on his phone. Then he exited the car with briefcase firmly in hand. The ambiance out of doors was equally intense parts of heat and light, but Richard held his gaze steady as he walked a few blocks and entered the shaded and sterile environs of the Ramcin Tower.

*

A security detail awaited inside, a more formidable and officious outfit than he'd previously encountered. They looked like reformed gangbangers or militants in stretchy black uniforms. On the silent elevator ride, Richard, behind his shades, studied their waists but did not detect any serious weapons among the cornucopia of security apparatus attached to their belts. Still, he'd worried all along about his probable need to escape. And these guys raised Richard's already high anxiety. But there was no turning back now.

Jerry DeLaBomba waited outside the elevator door. He looked as nervous as Richard felt, rubbing his hands, twitching a smile. He sent the security team away and ushered Richard to the conference table where they had first met one month ago, though it seemed like much longer to both men.

"So, just so were clear, before we go in," Jerry said, tapping the table. "No funny business, right?"

"Right," Richard said, taking off his sunglasses.

"Cause that money's been wired. Mona has the confirmation number. I just heard from her."

"Me, too."

"I gotta tell ya," Jerry said, a nervous laugh freighting his confession. "The guys upstairs didn't want to play ball on this one. The uncertainty made them nervous, you know? It's a cultural thing, I guess. They're business people. Numbers guys. Bernie himself had to personally go up there. My god, what a salesman. He had them eating out of his hands, selling them on the profit it would turn and how it would lead to more easy money in the cesspool of America. He actually said that, 'Cesspool of America.' I think they liked that."

Richard, too dizzied by other possibilities to focus on the conversation, didn't respond.

"Of course," Jerry continued, his face now sober. "Bernie knows, just like I do, that if this thing doesn't work out, we're all out the door.

We're done for good. We got a responsibility to make money for them upstairs. Every quarter. It's how corporations work. You don't blow this kind of money and somehow get a chance to make it back down the road. Know what I'm saying?"

Richard found himself annoyed, an unfamiliar emotion though one he embraced as a symbol of his new-found confidence. He wanted to get this moment moving, not have a conversation about fiduciary responsibility with a scumbag producer worried about his job.

"Why are we talking about this?" Richard asked.

"I dunno," Jerry mumbled. "I'm just looking for a little piece of mind before I bring you in there."

"I'm only an artist," Richard said, getting to his feet. "What do I know about these things?"

Jerry stood up and held took Richard by the forearm. "Just tell me these pictures are legit, alright?"

Richard looked into Jerry's eyes, behind the giant and thick frames. He suddenly felt empowered and completely unsympathetic. "They're legit," his said with absolute sincerity.

Jerry smiled every so slightly and let a gust of air out through his nose. "Let's go," he said, leading Richard down the hall towards the studio.

*

The studio was being staged for the show to begin shortly. Production assistants checked microphones. Panel boards flickered with red and green lights. The room was the same as Richard remembered, though the mood was tense. The buffet had hardly been touched. The room didn't smell much like coffee or food. The KBAL Crew were in their places, but no one spoke. Bernie sat on his thrown, behind the plexiglass, in a black rodeo shirt festooned with fake-jewel patterns, his eyes closed, a busty intern at his side, rubbing his temples. Sid flipped through a newspaper; Smoov scratched a stack of lottery tickets. Leonard Temple, sans dirty Dodgers cap and primped in a crisp white shirt opened at the collar, read through the show's agenda. Jerry DeLaBomba coughed to get their attention. Leonard was the first to turn around.

"My, my, my," he cooed, tucking a strand of hair behind his ear. "My prince has returned, in a sear sucker suit, no less. I feel like Julia Roberts in *Pretty Woman.*"

"Who says he's here for you?" Sid said with a cocky chuckle.

"A boy can dream, can't he?" Leonard responded without taking his eyes of of Richard.

Richard held up his hand as a bashful 'hello.' Then he pointed, in question, to the chair next to Leonard, which the host patted, a debonair, come-hither look blooming in his face. Jerry nudged Richard towards the table where Leonard sat and then stepped to the front of the room, his back to Bernie who had yet to open his eyes.

"OK," Jerry began, striking the focused-tone of a coach before a big game. "We go live in a few, and - I don't need to tell you - this is an important show. Upstairs is all over this one. Remember, they got cameras coming in to broadcast live on three channels, including one back home in China, where apparently this whole thing is just catching on, like an overnight sensation. So, do me a favor - keep the antics down. You guys are pros. Best in the business. Right?"

There was no reaction to the producer's prompt. The pep-talk look left his face.

"And if one of yas says 'Chink', I swear to God..."

Jerry's lack of conviction left him impotent and unable to muster up and more words. He stared absently around the room until the camera crew came in through the door. Jerry immediately approached them for a consultation. Sid and Smoov returned to their previous activities. Bernie dispatched his head masseuse and began stroking his cross bow, staring at Richard.

Richard retrieved his metal case and put it on the table in front of him. Leonard rolled his finger tips across the top of the case and leaned over to whisper in Richard's ear.

"So," he asked, in a lush tone. "Will we be getting our money's worth?"

Richard shrugged, a coy smile tugging the sides of his mouth.

"OK, Lover," Leonard purred. "I'm with you." He stared at Richard with a look both conspiratorial and omniscient.

Roman Candles went off behind Richard's eyes. All of this suddenly seemed like a lot of fun. It felt like destiny. He felt invincible, ready for whatever happened. He was walking out of that room soon, no matter what. And in that moment of clarity and triumph, another idea came to Richard, perhaps the most magnificent idea he'd ever had.

The lights flickered and a hush fell over the studio as the supporting staff scurried from the studio. Three cameras were in place: one on Richard and Leonard; one on Smoov and Sid; one on Bernie who had returned the crossbow to its rack and now sat imperiously on his throne, his head scanning the room as if he were looking over all the viewers privy to the camera feed. Postures were assumed by the other men in the room. Leonard rubbed his throat, coughed intentionally into his sleeve. Richard undid the latch on his case as the red light of the camera, directed at Leonard, began to flash.

"Welcome Angelinos, and Americanos, and, what I understand, is also an international audience on what is a live version of the program rewriting the rules of radio and, apparently, now television, as well, The Bernie Golden Show, featuring the KBAL crew of Mr. Sidney Fortunato and MC Smoov. I am of course, the program facilitator, Leonard Temple, who has the pleasure, five days a week, of getting the party started under the auspices of the G-Man himself, The Golden Child...Bernie Golden."

The music kicked in and Leonard's reverential yet sarcastic introduction was finalized by a mock-bow and hand spinning hand-gyration offered to the host.

The camera feed switched to Bernie, who stared stoically ahead then slowly turned his focus to the camera into which he carefully mouthed the word "Chink" before the feed returned to Leonard as he resumed the show's introduction.

"Today's show is obviously an important one, for we are joined - once again - by the charming and talented Mr. Richard Evans who has brought us some more photographic gems in his officious metal case. Isn't that right, dear Richard?"

"Yes," Richard said without pause and a certain sense of ease. "That's correct."

"Wonderful," Leonard responded. "But before we unpack today's treasures, brought to you by the coffers of Ramcin International, it might be appropriate to engage in a little retroactive foreplay, to remind our listeners, and our viewers, of course, around the world just what led us to this exalted position where we now sit, a scenario where two photographs of two celebrities will have been exchanged for a bounty that exceeds the GDP of most second world nations."

"Drop the soap and get off the box, Lenny," Bernie ordered with authority. He maintained a professional facade but was seething from the moment Leonard attributed the purchase of the picture to Ramcin. He had already sensed the betrayal and suspected subterfuge from the introduction monologue that smacked of sarcasm. He was beginning to suspect the two queers were in cahoots. He saw them whispering, exchanging furtive glances. Paranoia began to slither into Bernie's fragile psyche. He studied Sid and Smoov, who sat back in their chairs, arms crossed, disengaged from the dialog. Jerry D stood behind the glass in the production room, rubbing his arm and ready to sell out to the Chinks, if necessary. That's why he had to come upstairs and convince the Chinks to cut the check. And what was with that new security squad? They knew he was racist and especially contemptuous of black men. Were they sending him a message? He thought about that girl he had murdered in Nevada. Bernie's mind began to race as Leonard interrupted with a response to his demand.

"This is not a soapbox moment, I assure you, Mr. Boss, though it certainly deserves to be. What I am suggesting is a little context here to inform the narrative. This is a program, with a certain amount of time to fill. It is beholden on me, more than any one else, to provide the necessary breadth to our conversations. In this case, it seems appropriate for their to be a little some background and build up, some dramatic tension before we get to the epic reveal of this oh-so-important matter that you've so brilliantly orchestrated."

Leonard was spinning bullshit, Bernie knew, but he had no comeback. He couldn't shut him down with a standard slash, the audience was far too large; he had no support from Sid and Smoov, who were too fucking stupid to see what was happening. He'd have to stay cool and stay in the game. Play his hand.

"Have it your way, muchacho," Bernie said, a current of civility, even camaraderie, in his tone.

"Gracias," Leonard responded, with dramatic elocution. "It's important for our audiences, both here and abroad, to be aware that this narrative really didn't truly begin when Mr. Richard Evans walked into our studios with the photograph known as "Martinis & Bikinis." No, truly, this whole sad adventure began sometime much, much earlier, when artists among us became targets for intrusion and exploitation, when their personal lives became more interesting to us than their creative lives. Naturally, this slowly rendered much of their work unappreciated and facilitated not only an exile of artists, literally and figuratively, from our midst but a rise in stature of those far less talented but more amenable to said exploitation. And it continues to spiral downward, our aesthetic subject to the law of diminishing returns and expectations and standards. It has given rise to legions of lowest common denominator mediums, magazines and TV shows and radio programs where fortunes are amassed and mountains are moved through gossip and humiliation and unwanted or undeserved attention."

Richard could feel Leonard, despite his calm veneer and elegant speech, shaking. His glance was steely, but his breath was labored as he slouched at the shoulders and hovered above his microphone. He was speaking extemporaneously, but the narrative was one he had informally rehearsed many times. One he was clearly passionate about. Everyone was silent. Even Bernie Golden started straight ahead, seemingly unfazed by this unexpected commentary. The pause was slight, but uninterrupted, which encouraged Leonard to continue.

"The devil here is not show's like this one nor the multitude of other sources of garbage commonly recognized as entertainment these days. If I could paraphrase *The Usual Suspects*, a truly magnificent film from the halcyon days of the 90s, the greatest trick the devil ever played was convincing the world he didn't exist. That's precisely what's happened here, though the devil isn't a truly sinister individual, it is something far more benign on the surface, but reprehensible underneath, at least, when it comes to the arts."

Leonard paused to lick his lips, and Richard watched Jerry DeLaBomba, in the control room, cover his eyes.

"Corporations are the devil," he said without emotion. "They feed on consumers, on profits, with no sense of greater good. They are singular organisms, like sharks, swimming the ocean with the sole purpose of eating everything in sight. No other *raison' d'etre*. No conscience. No moral compass. These are soulless entities with profit as their only motive. This might be fine and good when it comes to commodities, erasers and gadgets and other cheap plastic toys and clothing made in sweatshops around the world, but art is not a commodity. Art is precious. It is water for our souls. Art is what reminds us of our humanity. It should be nurtured and cherished and criticized. It should be held to a very high standard since it is a reflection of our times and a validation of our existence. Corporations have ceased hold of our arts and have, as a result, made whopping profits while simultaneously making our society less humane. We live in the theater of the absurd, where talent has no direct correlation to success, and as a result we are devolving. Look around. Rome is burning, baby, and all we care about is gossip and scandal. Thank you Ramcin International. Thank you corporations everywhere for what you have done to our world."

Richard opened his case, as if on cue, and handed the two pictures to Leonard, who, with shaking hands, held them at the best distance for inspection. He took a deep breath to compose himself after the lengthy commentary. A look of mirth began to slowly spread over his face. He sat up, glanced at Richard, and returned his starry gaze to the pictures. "Bravo," he said. "Bravo."

Big Sid and Smoov got up from their table and gathered over Leonard's shoulder, peering like children at the pictures.

"I don't get it," Sid said. "What's the big deal?"

"Yeah, mang," Smoov concurred. "That ain't no bravo."

"Bring them here!" Bernie ordered.

Sid snatched the photos from Leonard's hand and, like a good minion, marched them up to the boss. The cameraman on Bernie picked up Sid on the way and positioned himself at an angle to the side of the throne.

Bernie held the photos like playing cards, splayed out across one hand. He simply stared. The camera focused on the pictures: one black and white; the other in color.

The black and white photo of low-resolution featured Jack Flaherty and Angelica Lightman standing side by side in front of a stucco wall, dressed in vintage clothes, his arm slung diagonally across her back, her fingers touching in front of her sternum. He is dressed almost entirely in dark: tight jeans and tight t-shirt under an unbuttoned collared shirt, a weathered fedora tilted towards one eye, a white handkerchief knotted neatly around his neck. She was dressed almost entirely in off-white: linen pants rolled at the heels, a linen blouse knotted at the naval, sleeves rolled to the elbow, hair parted in the middle and resting on her shoulders, a black scarf folded into a two-inch ribbon and fastened low across her forehead.

In the vivid color photo, the couple are lying on top of a sheet-covered bed. She wears a black blouse and blue jeans, hair spilled above her where her arms extend and join at the wrist. He is completely nude. Curled into her hip, a leg across her mid-section, his arms clutching her head as a kiss is emphatically planted on her left cheek.

"I don't get it," Sid repeated.

"Of course you don't, you imbecile," Leonard laughed. "It's homage, you see, to art, two photographs of celebrities' not taken to spite or to shame but for the sake of art. The black & white is mimicking the photo of Patti Smith and Robert Mapplethorpe that graced the cover of her memoir, *Just Kids*. The color photo remakes John Lennon and Yoko Ono from the cover of *Rolling Stone* magazine. The irony here is enough to kill a man." He held a hand over his heart and gave Richard the once over.

Richard's heart pounded as the reveal left him speechless and dry-mouthed. He studied Bernie Golden who continued to stare at his photos.

"So, like, what," Sid continued his speculation. "They posed for those pictures. So, like, this is is all a joke? And they was in on it?"

"Very good, Sidney," Leonard said, dripping sarcasm. "Someone award this cretin an honorary GED."

Richard slowly tipped open the metal case as Bernie Golden sat up and scanned the room.

"Big Sid," he ordered. "Smear the queer."

Sid set his widened-eyes on Richard and took a deep breath through his nose. Jerry D, from the control room, pounded on the window, his call of "No!!!" audible in the studio, but not enough to stop Sid's charge. Sid did stop, though, instantly, at the site of Richard's gun. A 9mm Glock, held steady in both hands, trained on Sid's solar plexus from a mere five yards away.

"Holy shit, mang!" Smoov said, standing up. "Motherfucker got a gun!"

"Don't move," Richard said to him, over his shoulder.

Both Sid and Smoov raised their hands.

"Good lord," Leonard quipped. "He's not going to rob you morons. It's Bernie's money he came for. And it's already been stolen. Isn't that right, G-Man?

"You were in on this, weren't you, faggot?" Bernie snarled at Leonard.

"I absolutely was not a part of this, though I wish I was. Either way, I will not pretend that I'm not thrilled and impressed, in equal parts. This has been the most artistic moment of the 21st century, and I'm honored to have been merely the narrator and a witness."

Bernie Golden stood up, the pictures scrunched in his hand, and stared contemptuously at Richard. The cameras focused on Richard as he turned the gun on Bernie.

"It's your money, right? Well then, on behalf of the arts programs of the greater Los Angeles public schools, I thank you."

Richard bent a small bow in Bernie's direction, then redirected the gun at Big Sid and spoke to Leonard. "You want to be part of this?"

"Pardon," Leonard retorted.

"Do you want to be part of this?"

"Do I."

"Then come with me."

"Where?"

"Got a few ideas."

"Now?"

Richard nodded, and Leonard sprang up from his seat.

Bernie kicked at his plexiglass partition. "Walk out of here with the queer bait and there's no coming back," he seethed, his face flush with hatred and shame.

Leonard looked at Bernie and summoned the disgust he'd held since accepting this awful fucking job. "Suck my pussy, bitch," he said with enough venom to kill a dragon.

The cameraman stumbled back a step. Sid blushed. Smoov laughed. And Bernie Golden sat down on his throne and shook his head contemptuously, choking on desperation and outrage.

Richard, with the gun down and his eyes on Leonard, motioned with his head towards the door. The two men exited the room. In the corridor, Richard held the gun to his side and strolled alongside Leonard towards the landing.

"Was that even loaded?" Leonard asked suspiciously as they waited for the elevator.

"Yep," Richard responded as he removed the clip and fastened the pistol in his waist belt.

"Fabulous," Richard purred as the elevator door opened and the security detail charged past them towards the studio.

The two men rode the elevator down to the lobby in silence. They walked, unmolested, through the air conditioned lobby of Ramcin Tower. A rogue cloud blocked the sun as they exited the building and walked towards the waiting limousine.

Walter, stuffed into a dark suit with a pilot's hat and aviator glasses, held open the doors. "Nice job, mate," he said officiously as Richard followed Leonard into the backseat.

Walter closed the door and hustled around to the driver's side. The long car chirped the concrete and moved briskly down W. Victory Boulevard to the side street where it made an abrupt stop beside a rusted Honda Civic next to an Azalea patch swarming with humming birds.

Richard got out and Leonard followed. They climbed into the Civic, and Richard retrieved the keys and started the engine.

"So, where *are* we going?" Leonard asked.

"I was thinking Mexico City or Vancouver. You pick."

Leonard petted his cleft chin and pondered, "Hmmm. Let me see..." he said as Richard put the car in gear and headed towards the exits of Los Angeles.

*

Back in the studio, the security detail pounded on the door which Big Sid, on order from Bernie, had locked and barricaded with all the movable items in the room. The cameras continued to roll as Bernie Golden sought redemption in what he knew were his last moments of celebrity life. He looked with contempt into the camera and spoke with in a low, detached manner.

"The joke's not on me, America. No. No. No. This is not on me at all. It's on you. Don't you see, those dollars that those blood sucking Chinks upstairs blew on these fucking photographs all came from you. You gave it to them, hand over fist."

The pounding on the door grew louder and wood began to split. The mountain of furniture and bric-a-brac, which now included Sid and Smoov, pushing back on the pile, began to give way. The rest of the production crew, including Jerry LeLaBomba, stayed put in the control room, doing their jobs as if this were a regular show.

Bernie motioned for the camera on him to come closer. He leaned forward from his throne and stared deeply into the lens. "Our time here is short, America. The Chinks are coming; the Chinks are coming; the Chinks are coming. So I leave you, pathetic America, with a grand finale, one like I've had in mind during this entire charade. Since this whole show began as a joke on you. And now I bring to you the ultimate 'Golden Shower' - you've earned it America."

Bernie Golden stood up and gritted his teeth as he tore the $50 million pictures into pieces and dropped them in the toilet. He took his time unzipping his pants then turned his profile to the camera with his penis hidden in his hand angled towards the shredded scraps in the basin of the bowl. There was a pause for a few seconds as nothing happened. The noise from the door increased and Big Sid screamed as the pile came crashing down on him. The security outfit, about a dozen black men in dark clothes, trampled over Sid and Smoov as they stormed for Bernie. He closed his eyes as the urine arrived, a steady stream the soaked the pictures just before he was overwhelmed from behind.

*

The epic humiliation of Bernie Golden, and his subsequent thrashing at the hands of the security outfit, part of which was caught on film, became the immediate conversation in America. The video went viral, amassing millions of views and shutting down servers nationwide before the news broadcasts could even interrupt their regular programming to cover the story, which was being re-branded as "the hoax of the century," "David vs. Goliath" and "the return of Robin Hood." Social Media sites crashed, as well. A sense of frenzy enveloped the nation which was unable to reconcile this jarring event, both sensational and humbling. Rumors spread: Bernie Golden was dead; Jack Flaherty was connected to the Boston mafia; the money had been shipped to an offshore account.

The first fire was reported at 5:00 PST. It was set in the Hollywood Hills and quickly spread through the arid canyons, sweeping up the slopes towards the iconic sign. Residents began to evacuate in droves, but the highways couldn't accommodate all the traffic, already snarled by rush hour volume, prompting a city-wide panic which lead to riots, gunfire and blood on the streets of fantastic LA.

Copycat fires sparked up around the southwest, in Texas and Oklahoma. Soon, the Midwest and mountain regions, too, Iowa and Missouri and Colorado, had fires local resources could not contain. Governors begged for the National Guard to be activated, but the President refused to act, citing measures of austerity required to keep the spiraling national debt under control as well as the recent troop build up for the upcoming surge in the Middle East. Local first responders had been so depleted by budget cuts there simply was not enough man power to contain the fires, which would gain in intensity as night fell and the winds picked up.

*

At a night club in Boston, Jack's cousin Jeannie took the stage with the rest of her band. The stage was high and the lights were up, making it hard to see into the crowd. She'd been backstage, sequestered in the green room, suffering from anxiety that her band mates erroneously attributed to a newly acquired case of stage fright or diva syndrome. But Jeannie was not afraid of being on stage nor was she becoming a diva; she was afraid of the handsome yet damaged soldier who stared at her with pleading eyes as she performed recent gigs up and down the eastern seaboard. He wasn't at their last gig in Charlottesville, VA, and she secretly hoped he'd been redeployed to the Middle East, and she hated herself for hoping such an awful fate upon anyone, but he unnerved her in such a visceral way, as if she could feel his pain and sense it surfacing in perhaps a violent way. She felt such empathy for him, so much so that he sensed it in her and made her an object of his fascination. Jeannie nearly felt clairvoyant, as if she knew what he was wrestling with, the demons that haunted him behind his eyes that stared at her without emotion, though she somehow knew that he was going to act.

And there he was, at a night club in Boston ironically named The Middle East. Jeannie was swaying, strumming her guitar chords which began the third song in their set. He was in full fatigues, patches of beige, his hair freshly clipped under a sand-colored military cap. He stood straighter in his uniform, more erect, though the look was the same. The crowd gave him berth, standing a few feet away from him on all sides. And when Jeannie saw him, a guitar string snapped and whipped her cheek, as she began to gently weep.

*

On a nearby rooftop, Jack Flaherty and Angelica Lightman stared over the shimmering Boston skyline dimmed by looming clouds. They were surrounded by the detritus of their makeshift bedroom, the place where they'd been sleeping during the warm New England autumn as they hid from the media in the wake of "Martinis & Bikinis." Before Richard Evans' first appearance on the Bernie Golden Show, they'd successfully sequestered themselves in Jack's basement apartment with enough provisions to ride out the few weeks needed for the entire plan to be actuated. They removed themselves from all communication and committed to isolation until the call was made to a newly acquired cellphone which would be solely used for this purpose only.

They'd been at the sprawling modern home beyond Neverland Ranch on the California highlands north of Santa Barbara when Walter had arrived at the front door that faced the long and winding drive up an isolated mountain. Jack answered the knock in a bathing suit and not a word was exchanged with Walter, only a sheepish look that convinced Jack to fetch Angelica, who reluctantly came to the door in a sarong and t-shirt over her wet bathing suit. Standing on the landing, shaded by palm trees, facing the couple in the threshold, Walter offered a blubbering apology for his betrayal. His jaw still freshly broken, he mumbled in agony about the agony he felt emotionally for his role in the deception. He explained his relationship with Mona November and her relationship to the film, and that her motives were inspired by a desperation for *The Killing Kind* to be a success since her future as a screenwriter of important films lie in the balance. She also wanted to see the film succeed so the production company could continue its important work. The reveal of Mona as the clandestine screenwriter struck a chord with Angie, as a woman and an artist, as did the sincerity of Walter's apology. Besides, he was her dear cousin after all, and a loyal and dutiful companion and protector since her days in England. At this point in her life, he was the only family she had left. After a fitful hug with Angie and a forgiving handshake with Jack, Walter begged for them to stay calm; he had someone waiting in the car who meant them absolutely no harm, but instead had a potentially brilliant idea he wanted to share.

Angie gasped when Walter returned from the car with a stranger carrying a camera. Richard held the camera benignly in his hands as a means of association, of context, hoping he would be recognized easier by Jack, his former neighbor in the apartment building near the Santa Monica/Brentwood border from years back and the one, the night before, who had refused to snap his photo on the red carpet outside Man's Chinese Theater. Jack calmed Angie with an arm around her shoulder as he pointed casually at Richard.

"2nd floor. Corner," he said. "Right?"

Richard nodded. He wanted to smile; he wanted to speak, but he felt unsteady, unsure of himself, his feet feeling as if he's stepped on an idle escalator. His mouth went dry, and he didn't know how to begin.

"Come inside," Jack suggested. "And we'll go out back."

They walked through the spacious foyer well-lit by faint light of early dusk that poured through the skylights and floor-to-ceiling windows that looked over the pool in back. On the slate patio that surrounded the pool, bordered by a hedge of imported Cypress trees, they sat on chaise lounges around a small glass table topped by a sweating pitcher of vodka and two martini glasses. Richard's idea originally included only the homage to the Smith/Mapplethorpe and Ono/Lennon photos, but the poolside cocktails and couple in their bathing suits reminded him of his favorite album from the 90s, and gave him the language to launch his proposal.

"Have you ever heard of Sam Phillips?"

Jack shook his head. Angie blinked in recognition. "The pop singer?" she asked.

"Exactly," Richard said, "though I wouldn't call it pop."

"And she also, somehow, appeared beside Bruce Willis in one of those *Die Hard* sequels," Angie added. "Remember that?"

Walter raised his hand.

"Me, too," Richard acknowledged, with a cringe, "but let's forget about the whole *Die Hard* thing and focus on her album *Martinis & Bikinis*."

"What about it?" Angie asked.

Richard shared his idea. His entire plan, now reconfigured on the spot, an artistic improvisation worthy of the best jazz musician, a blend of the spontaneous and the rehearsed, a suite in two parts beginning with the poolside photograph and followed - at some point later - by the dual photos honoring royal artists/couples. The first part would be the set up; the second the reveal. And the reveal would be a gigantic knee to the nuts of the entire entertainment exploitation complex.

Angie was aghast. "And why in the hell would I, or we even, want more attention?"

"It might get intense for a little," Richard confessed, "but, ultimately, it could make a difference in your life, and in the lives of artists everywhere."

"And how's that?" she begged.

"By making a statement about artists and art, and how they are to be respected by society, not exploited. It will hold up a mirror to the failure of American media in the age of corporate imposition into nearly phase of society."

"A bit grandiose," Angie quipped. "And moralistic. Don't you think?"

"Yes," Richard said without pause or shame.

Angie leaned back in her chaise lounge, lit a cigarette and blew smoke at a sky that horded the last bits of dying light. A bald eagle circled high over head. A champagne glow sifted down upon the untamed canyons and barren ridges of the central California coastline, upon the unlikely foursome who considered the possibilities of a daring idea.

"Anybody hungry?" Jack broke the silence to inquire.

Walter raised his hand. Richard offered a wan smile as Angie continued to stare at the sky. A makeshift table was set as Jack prepared lamb chops "Scottadito" to be singed on the grill and eaten by hand as Walter mixed fresh cocktails in the pool house wet bar. After cocktails, the four of them ate poolside and drank California wine long into a California night rung with stars. Coyotes howled from the hilltops as they talked about a myriad of topics all related tangentially or directly to Richard's idea and the statement it could possibly make. Or not. And eventually, Angie set up beds for the unexpected guests and a decision was made to move forward with the plan.

The next morning Richard and Walter drove to a vintage clothing shop in Santa Barbara and returned with outfits that closely resembled those worn by Patti Smith and Robert Mapplethorpe on the cover of Smith's memoir. No purchases were necessary to emulate the other photo. With clothes in hand, or not, the pictures were easy to take.

The poolside shot was more difficult, as light was imperative along with the impression that Richard was shooting from a distance and in duress. But Richard's talent made it a relatively short shoot, and the foursome had to debate which picture was the best during another night of cocktails, conversation and dinner.

The next day, Walter dropped Jack and Angie at the Burbank Airport. They took a chartered flight to Boston and a cab to Jack's basement apartment in the empty Back Bay mansion where they sequestered themselves until the cellphone, which would arrive from Mona via FedEx a few days after their arrival, eventually rang. Nine days later, in the early evening, as Jack and Angie played chess on the floor, the forgotten phone buzzed on the kitchen counter.

"Done," is all the text message read.

"A bit cloak and dagger," Angie commented "Don't you think?"

Jack shrugged and went back to the chess game. Angie retrieved her tablet from isolation and powered it on. They learned of the days events: The photographs had fetched $50 million, courtesy of Ramcin International. Richard has escaped the studio in the company of Leonard Temple. Their whereabouts unknown. Bernie Golden was in a coma. Hollywood was burning. So were parts of six other states. Riots broke out in three major cities and on the freeways of Los Angeles. A soldier had committed suicide at a Boston nightclub. And a massive snow storm, dubbed "The Gynorma-Nor'easter" was slated to bring gale force winds, coastal flooding and a record shattering snowfall to most of New England.

Jack and Angie retreated to the roof from where the lights of Boston flickered like silver coins and the first of the snow began faintly falling down.

THE END

www.ingramcontent.com/pod-product-compliance
Lightning Source LLC
Chambersburg PA
CBHW022000120726
47992CB00001B/341